The 21 Lives of Sanjay and Cider

Written by Joseph D Lyman

With Illustrations by Sariah Lyman

Poems by Malachi Lyman
Cover art by Stephanie Lyman
Edited by Samuel Lyman

ISBN: 978-1-7363739-2-7

Library of Congress Control Number: 2023911102

Pinpoint Management, LLC. Fulton, Missouri

To my sensational kids, Sariah, Sam, and Malachi, who laugh at my nonsense and encourage me to write more of it; and to the love of my life, Stephanie, who makes everything worthwhile.

Thus are the 21 lives...

Introduction

You can write for an audience, or you can write for yourself, or you can write for profit. Perhaps in rare instances you may be able to write for all three. This book was written for my family.

I mention this so the reader will know what they are getting into. The stories herein are for a very particular crowd. It's an audience that I know well, an audience that I love, and an audience that is capable of translating my entire character into the stories I tell them. In other words, it's a rare audience, the kind that loves me and forgives me before they read a single word; the best kind.

These stories—which revolve around two semi-consistent main characters who find themselves in a variety of existences—were written primarily to amuse my audience. In general, the first drafts were written in an evening, often in response to prompts provided by the family, and read aloud that same evening. Imagine a dad, his wife and kids, and a few sheets of paper, in a cozy living room somewhere—then you'll be in the right mood to read these properly.

The order of the stories is strange. Granted, there is no obvious, intrinsic order that they should fall into; but that being the case, one might reasonably expect that they would at least be sorted in a fashionable order, or in a logical order, or in a pleasing order. For my part, I wanted to put some of the stories I liked best in the front, so that readers would be more likely to finish the book. But alas, they are sorted chronologically by the date they were written and read aloud to my family, who would have it no other way. I must please them. They are my audience, after all.

As for the characters—Sanjay and Cider—their words and deeds and actions will speak for themselves. You'll know them as children, as friends, as enemies, as co-workers, as animals, as toys, as angels, as swindlers, and as pure logic. These situations aren't designed to convey much beyond what you find on the surface; they're just containers. In and through all of these shells of imagined existence, you'll find threads of personality, which are the essence.

To my family and to anyone else who stumbles upon them, I happily and gratefully give you *The 21 Lives of Sanjay and Cider*.

City Beyond the Pass

No one quite knows what happens
When this life flies past
What place we go to when we die
In the ground or sea or sky,
And we move on at last.
What will it be like to see or feel?
What things can we do
(I don't think we'll just sing)
Can we make things from thin air?
Will we live without care?
Yes, no one quite knows what the next life will
bring.
– Malachi Lyman

This is a story about a man and his horse. Anyone who knows about these kinds of stories—the kind with men and horses—knows that the horse is just as important as the man. Sometimes you might wonder how the story would have turned out if the horse was in charge, instead of his rider. This is one of those times.

Sanjay rode atop his trusty horse, Cider. Sanjay was named after his father; Cider was named for the lustrous gold-amber color of his coat. The path they trod was a familiar one; for years they had traveled the trade road between two cities that have long since been lost to history. One was a lush ocean-side destination, full of spices and wealth; the other was a distant desert crossroads full of travelers, among them rich envoys of princes, czars, and sultans.

Cider knew the path like he knew his own feed bag (which was almost all he thought about as they walked). Sanjay knew the people and their desires like he knew the seat of his saddle, where he spent countless tiresome hours as they trotted through the vast, empty desert.

Their saddle bags laden with exotic spices coming from the ocean-side city and bound for the desert crossroads, Sanjay and Cider approached the mid-point in their journey, a watering spot of some renown. The blessed resting place was in distant sight, when an impetuous and powerful wind rose from the east without warning. At first they pushed on, Sanjay reassuring Cider as they went.

"We've been through worse, haven't we old friend?"

Cider didn't answer, but bent his head down and increased his pace. After all, that watering spot wasn't too much further.

The wind continued to increase, the dust and sand kicking up in startling bursts. Sanjay, whose voice was beginning to falter, tried again to bolster their spirits.

"It's just a bit of dust. Nothing we can't handle, right old boy?"

Still no answer from his friend. The trot was forced down to a walk by the sheer strength of the wind, but still they pressed on.

Finally, as the sand beat hard against them both and visibility was reduced to just a few dozen staffs, Sanjay was forced to admit defeat. He clicked loudly with his tongue, and pulled the reigns to the west. Cider, seeing where they were headed, tugged back toward the direction of the watering hole.

"Oh, come on now Cider, you don't believe those stories! Come, The Pass—"

Sanjay was about to say "The Pass of the Dead", but decided against referencing the place's common name.

"The rocks of that pass over there will provide some shelter. We can't stay in this storm, Cider, can we? Come on, hurry along!"

He prodded his friend's flank with his boot, and snapped the reigns. He knew his horse would eventually comply, but felt a sense of urgency. The sand was stinging his eyes, and dehydration from the dusty wind was burning his throat.

In a short while, they reached the pass, but the wind was as hard as ever. Somehow, the gusts felt like they were blowing from all directions—in front, from above, and from behind— all at the same time. Sanjay even felt like it was blowing up from the ground and into his pant legs. The dust and sand were so thick, they couldn't see more than a single staff length in front of them.

Sanjay's head swam. He hadn't had water for far too long. He longed for relief—from his thirst, and from the storm— but the smooth rock walls offered no shelter, and he had left the watering hole behind. He tried to keep his head down and urge Cider on, but eventually, he fainted.

He was only out a moment. When he came to, he felt a renewed strength and conviction. He shouted out, snapped the reigns hard, and brought Cider to a gallop.

It felt as if they were outrunning the wind, but Sanjay knew that it was just the storm letting up. He could see ahead to what looked like an opening in the pass. Finally, a few moments later, a large swish signaled the end of the storm, just as they passed the last outcropping of the rocky passage.

Cider came to a halt, and the two paused and caught their breath.

Ahead lay a vista that neither had set eyes on before. An expansive plain covered with golden fields of grain opened before them, waving gently in the setting sun. At the edge of the fields, just visible in the distance, was a great city surrounded by a deep-red wall.

"I bet they have water there."

That was all Cider needed to hear.

The walk was long, but the two eventually reached the city. By the time they were at the gate, a rabble of children from the fields were trailing behind them, talking in whispers. Sanjay looked up to find a guard he could hail in the towers, but there were none to be seen.

"Well, how do they expect us to get in?"

Just as he posed this question to Cider, the gate clanked, and began to slowly grind open.

As it turned out, the sultan of this great city was just on his way outside the gates, to gaze on his farmland. The guards had been distracted clearing the way inside the gate, for his passage.

On seeing Sanjay and Cider, one of the particularly fussy guards scoffed, and was about to send them into the ditch with his whip, when the sultan raised his hand.

"Guards—bring that man to me."

They obeyed. Sanjay, who was used to dealing with the envoys of sultans, didn't know enough to be afraid. He bowed low on his horse, and gave a customary greeting.

"And who are you?" asked the sultan in response.

"I am Sanjay, and this is Cider, Your Majesty. We have come from the ocean, to trade at the crossroads, but got caught in a storm at the pass."

The sultan seemed amused.

"And what, traveler, is it that you carry for the trade?"

Sanjay reached back and unlatched a bag. The sultan's guards lowered their spears.

"It is spices, my Lord," Sanjay quickly explained. "I carry some of the finest spices in the southern country."

"Spices! My word, we haven't seen a spice trader here in ages!"

The sultan clapped. In moments his envoy had turned about, and he had Sanjay and Cider guided into the city by his own guards. Sanjay couldn't believe it—he was actually leading the sultan! Sanjay had never been so honored. For a moment, he forgot his thirst, his tired back, and even the sand in his pants.

Before long, the sultan had taken him to the palace, where he and Cider were given food, drink, and fresh clothing. Though the food and drink were exquisite, the clothes were foreign and unfamiliar.

"I look like one of those performers from the far countries, who sometimes come to the market—a juggler perhaps" Sanjay thought to himself. He considered changing back into his dusty garments, but quickly put the idea out of his mind. If these were the clothes the sultan wished to provide, then these were the clothes he should wear.

After they were both cleaned and rested, Sanjay and Cider were led out of the palace, and into the evening market.

"The sultan awaits—he would like to see your wares," a guard informed him.

The market was more rich and bustling than any Sanjay had ever experienced. He swallowed hard—certainly, he could have nothing that these people would be lacking!

The guards guided him to a spot in the market that appeared to have been cleared especially for him. The sultan was waiting, a small crowd of wealthy merchants gathered around him.

"Ah, he is here! The spice merchant!"

The sultan clapped. When the sultan claps, everyone claps twice as hard, and so all of the merchants cheered for Sanjay and Cider.

Feeling more sheepish than ever, Sanjay dismounted, and started to unpack. First, he took down his rug. He had never felt bad about his rug before, but he was worried that it might be too dusty, too old, and too simple for such a market as this. He unrolled it, and laid it down, smoothing it out as best he could.

The sultan and the merchants looked on, smiling.

Next, he took down his saddle bags. Cider neighed nervously as the bags were removed. The bags were of thick, sturdy leather, and heavily laden with spices. He carefully removed several wooden bowls, and arranged them according to his skill as a trader. He laid out bag after bag of precious and rare spices, filling the bowls part way, to reveal his treasure's color and smell. As soon as he was done, he sat down.

The sultan approached.

"I have never seen a more beautiful display of spices! We have many treasures here, but the cultivation of spices is beyond our skill..."

"Behold!" he said, turning to the merchants, "the most celebrated spice trader in the land!"

The merchants clapped and cheered. As soon as the sultan stepped aside, they rushed upon Sanjay. He could hardly hear their offers, but it hardly mattered—they were heaving gold, silver, jewels and mystical items upon him in exchange for his spices, and no price seemed too high. Before he could counter their offers, they offered more.

"I'll give you seven gold pieces—no, take this gold platter! You can see your reflection in it, and with it you can summon the image of anyone, anywhere!"

"Take this gem! It was found in the center of a Peach of Immortality, and grants long life to whoever holds it!"

"This silver goblet will fill with the sweetest water, on command! Take it! Take it!"

Sanjay could not believe his fortune. Cider could not believe it either. He stomped his feet anxiously.

Soon, the whole market was abuzz over Sanjay's visit. Every merchant had come—Sanjay wondered how he would carry his haul, and was even forced to barter for more leather bags, which the merchants were glad to exchange for his apparently rare spices.

All this time, Cider was growing more and more uneasy. At first, Sanjay thought that perhaps he was worried about the prospect of having to carry everything (gold being so much heavier than spices), but eventually Sanjay began to feel uneasy as well. Deep inside, Sanjay knew that Cider was always right about these sorts of feelings.

Finally, he sold his last spices, and began to hurriedly pack up.

"You will stay and celebrate with us, yes?"

It was the sultan, who had approached as the merchants dispersed.

"Well, I would like that, kind sultan, but—"

Sanjay searched for an excuse.

"But, I have already made a trade with a distant merchant, which I must hasten to honor."

Sanjay knew the sultan would understand. A trader's word is very important.

"I understand. Well, I think you can stay just one night! Come, we will dine, and you will know the comfort of a palace!"

"I would like that, oh gracious sultan," Sanjay said again nervously, "but in truth Your Majesty, I ought not. You see, I promised to be there this very night."

The sultan frowned. First it was about Sanjay's word, but now it was about a promise. And a sultan knows that you simply can't break a promise.

"Go then first to the palace, so that you may change into your own clothing, which my servants have cleaned and prepared. Then you may have my leave."

Without another word, but with several more frowns, the sultan turned and stomped off.

Sanjay finished packing up the bags, then hopped on Cider and headed for the city gate.

"I don't trust him. I don't want to get stuck here, Cider, not even for a night. The king can keep my clothing, these things I have on will be just fine."

As he approached the gate, the guards, who recognized him as the one who had been so favored by the sultan, immediately opened the large doors.

As he passed through into the now dark fields and toward the pass, Sanjay felt a wave of relief. With about a hundred staffs between him and the city he was starting to feel that everything would be alright, when he heard a shout. The guards were bustling, and the gate was being opened.

"After him! Thief! Cheat! Bandit!"

You must understand, Sanjay only dealt in the highest quality spices. He had been called many things before, and while he didn't mind being called thief or bandit, he resented being called a cheat, because he knew that he certainly had not lied about his spices. Was it his fault if the people of this crazy city wanted to exchange their treasures for his simple offerings? It was supply and demand, not theft!

Sanjay suddenly forgot his hurt pride as the heavy trample of war horses reached his ear from within the city wall. He whipped Cider into a gallop (he didn't really have to; Cider knew what to do, but Sanjay couldn't help it) and they headed like mad for the pass. Behind him, he heard more shouts as the lead horseman shot out of the gate.

"Stop! Come back with those, they aren't yours! You mustn't!"

As they rode across the road and through the fields, another storm began to blow. The dust seemed to slow the armor-clad soldiers more than it did him and Cider, and soon Sanjay had reached the pass. By the time they were between the rock walls, the wind and dust and sand were just as bad as they had been when they arrived. They slowed to a walk, with a staff's distance visible before them. Then, Sanjay fainted for the second time that day.

When he came to it was morning. He was exiting the pass on Cider's back, moving at a crawl. The storm was letting up, and they were both covered in dust and sand. His throat was once again parched, his eyes were once again stinging, and the events of the city beyond the pass danced like a strange dream in his mind.

"Did that really happen, Cider?" he asked in a dry rasp that was barely audible.

He was limp in the saddle. Luckily, Cider knew the way, and carried them onward to the watering spot.

As they arrived and Cider dipped his head to the cool water, Sanjay fumbled out of the saddle and fell to his knees. He crawled to the waters edge and began furiously cupping that life-giving liquid to his mouth in great splashing gulps. He drank until he started to feel sick to his stomach, then he collapsed, rolled onto his back, and fell asleep.

Before too long, other travelers arrived at the popular spot. Cider nudged Sanjay with his nose until he awoke. Startled and instantly alert, he immediately recognized the voices of his fellow traders, Akash and Hasan.

"Friends!" he cried out, "I have had a singular vision, as I passed through that storm just now!"

The two looked confused.

"Akash! Hasan! Come close, that I might tell you all I have dreamed, and you may tell me what it meant!"

The two jumped together when their names were spoken.

"Ho there traveler," Akash said from afar, "tell us your name, and how you come to know us!"

Sanjay stood up.

"It is your old friend, Sanjay! Perhaps you did not recognize me for all the dust!"

Sanjay looked down at his clothes, and saw they were not his clothes, but the odd juggler's clothes that the sultan had given him. His friends, clearly disturbed, dug their heels into their horses and galloped off.

"Wait, come back!"

He shouted after them, but they were gone. Then, it hit him.

"But—but this must mean that it was not a dream! It was real!"

His mind flew instantly to the treasure. He turned to his saddle bags and wrestled the clasp open, throwing back the leather cover. A horde of glistening gold, silver, and jewels beamed back at him. He took hold of the silver goblet.

"They said it would fill on command," he said to Cider. As soon as the word "fill" left his lips, cool, clear water rose from the bottom to the brim. He drank it down.

"Amazing!"

Digging in the sack, he pulled out the mystical gold platter and eyed it with wonder. It reflected a face which he had never seen. He dropped the platter and shuddered. The reflection was not his own.

Disbelief and horror set in, and he scooped up the platter to check it again. There, staring back at him, was an older gentleman with a large mustache; a performer's face to match a performer's clothes. The odd visage imitated when Sanjay moved, smiled, blinked, or frowned. It was his face, yet it was not.

A thought struck him.

"They said it would show me anyone, anywhere! I wish to see myself—I mean Sanjay, the trader!"

He gazed into the mirror-finish of the platter and watched as his stranger's-reflection swirled and was replaced with the image of a young man lying motionless in a deserted pass flanked by steep, rocky cliffs. He had seen it before: It was the pass of the dead.

He closed his eyes for a moment, then quietly put the plate back in the bag. As he moved things around to make room, he noticed a large gem, pink and orange and glistening.

"What did he say? The Peach of Life? Immortality?"

He removed the gem and turned it over in his hands.

"I don't think we can go back, Cider."

He sighed, then looked up at the sky.

"But, I think we have everything we need to go forward. Come, let us continue on this journey that we call Life; and let us be more wise this time about where we go and what we do there."

Cider nodded and neighed in agreement.

Dah Megnat!

"'After all,' Anne had said to Marilla once, 'I believe the nicest and sweetest days are not those on which anything very splendid or wonderful or exciting happens but just those that bring simple little pleasures, following one another softly, like pearls slipping off a string.' "
– L. M. Montgomery, Anne of Avonlea

Plowing a field is hard work for the body, but simple work for the mind. It should come as no surprise, therefore, that a farmer might be pondering on the complexities of life as he worked. After all, he could only think for so long about the money he lost while playing cards with his friends the previous evening. Eventually, weightier matters must take their proper place.

This day—gray, late-winter, lonely and quiet—was a particularly ponderous sort of day. It was just the sort of day that Sanjay would choose for putting furrows in his field. His hard-working horse, Cider, knew the routine almost by heart, he had done it so many times. Up and down they went, over the hard patch of earth they called simply, The Farm. Occasionally they would stop for a break, which Cider would use to nibble at bits of weed and dead grass, while Sanjay would lean against him and rest.

When he was in a good mood, Sanjay would start up a conversation.

"Cider, my old friend, what do you think the weather will do this year?" He would sometimes ask. Or, he might say something like, "Cider, steering this plow is back-breaking work!", forgetting that pulling the plow was even more laborious.

But today, Sanjay just stood there and sighed. After sighing he'd wait a few moments, kick at the dirt and then sigh some more. Cider chewed quietly, but kept watch on his friend out of the corner of his eye. Finally, unable to sigh his thoughts and wishes away (oh how he longed to be anywhere but The Farm!) no matter how hard he tried, Sanjay turned to go back to his plow, when something caught his attention.

There before him was a sort of mirror—at least, he thought it was a mirror at first. The problem was that unlike a well-behaved mirror, there was no wall for it to hang on. It was a large oval, about the size of a dressing mirror, and it floated in the air a few yards in front of him.

Sanjay took a step closer and stopped. He had learned years ago to approach new things very slowly.

He could see now that the mirror didn't quite reflect things the way a mirror ought. Instead of a perfect picture, he saw light and shape and color that seemed to be like the light and shape and color around him, but not quite.

He took another step closer. Nothing bad happened, so he took another step, and another. Soon, he was next to the strange object. It was, indeed, a very ill-behaved mirror. Instead of a solid piece of glass, it appeared to perhaps be made of some sort of thick liquid. It quivered in the chilly air, much as Sanjay sometimes did, especially when he was thinking of something creepy.

Cider, noting that his master was approaching this strange new object with great caution, was not worried. Horses have sense, as everyone knows, and Cider had sense enough to let his master do what he wanted.

Having seen all that there was to see in his examination of the object, Sanjay was ready to move on to a more tangible probe. He plucked a blade of dead grass from the ground and extended it slowly toward the mirror. As it met the splashy looking glass, instead of doing any of the practical things a blade of grass might do when it touches a mirror (even a watery one), the grass simply passed into it. Sanjay pulled it back out and examined it; it was still a normal blade of grass. He pushed it into the mirror again, this time further. He wiggled it around, and pulled it back out.

"I'm getting nowhere this way," he said to Cider, who was so used to his random comments that he didn't even look up from his snack.

Sanjay decided it would be safe to try another experiment. Rolling up his sleeve, he extended a single finger toward the mirror. To his surprise, his finger passed into the mirror just as the blade of grass had done, and he didn't even feel a thing! He put his whole hand in, and still felt nothing.

Finally, he stood right next to the floating anomaly, and looked at the other side while passing his hand through—and found that he could not see his hand on the other side.

Sanjay fell back in alarm. Cider lifted his head and neighed at the disruption.

"Cider, you'll not believe this!" he said.

Dusting himself off, he looked at the mirror once more.

"I just don't get it. Where does my hand go, then, if not through to the other side?"

He thought for a few moments, as he walked slowly around the floating mirror.

"Perhaps if I could look inside," he mused, " I could find the answer."

Slowly, he leaned into the mirror. First, his nose went through, and he felt nothing. Then, the rest of his face followed, as it naturally would, and Sanjay found himself standing there, staring at an empty late-winter field, only half plowed.

"This is nonsense!" he said, pulling his head back.

He turned to face his friend, but Cider was not there.

"Cider!" he cried out, thinking that perhaps he had wandered off to a better snacking location.

There was no response. He wandered around the field, all the way down to the edge of the woods, then over to the creek, but there was no Cider.

"Blast that lazy beast!" he said, unfairly. For it was Cider who did most of the farm work.

In his heart, Sanjay was concerned for his friend. He hurried up to the house, his head bent low in consternation. As he approached the back yard, he looked up, to see if he could spot Cider at the barn.

Sanjay stopped in his tracks. He did a double take. This was not his house, though he wished that it was. This house was clean and neat, and everything, including the annoying old leaky window sill, was in tip-top shape.

"Cider!" he cried, looking all around.

Just then, a man came out the back door. He was large, well-dressed, and ill-humored. He shouted something unintelligible, and pointed toward Sanjay's clothes. Sanjay looked down at his work attire, which was covered in dirt.

"Sir, I'm sorry to bother you—" he started, but the man stepped back into his home, shouting something that sounded quite alarming as he slammed his door. Sanjay could see through the window that he was retrieving a shotgun from above the hutch. He scampered off around the house directly, deciding that it might be better to go look for Cider on the public road.

The road, too, was unfamiliar. It was well-used, but neatly graded, devoid of debris, and covered with a fresh layer of gravel—in short, it was nothing like the old roads around his house. He followed it along, with no sign of his friend, until he came to a small town. As he walked down the center of the main street, Sanjay whistled low. Every shop and every boardwalk looked freshly painted, spotlessly clean, and in perfect order. Men and women, dressed in their finest, walked about with the slow sort of ease that only the truly wealthy enjoy.

Finally, he came to what looked like a tack shop. He entered through the large carriage doors, looking for the proprietor.

"Hello? Is anyone in? I'm looking for my horse," he ventured into the dimly lit shop.

In a moment, a man appeared from around a corner. Upon seeing Sanjay, he cried out in disgust, with words that sounded to Sanjay like, "Glerv! Skin dee vivit! Dah! Dah megnat!"

"Excuse me, what was that?"

"Dah!"

The man had approached, and was now pushing Sanjay backward out the door.

"Sir! There's no need for all that!"

"Dah! Eek den bizat! Dah megnat!"

By this time, the man had muscled Sanjay out into the road, and ended by pushing him over onto the ground. A small crowd began to gather.

"I'm only looking for my horse! We were plowing in the field, and he wandered off!"

The people were murmuring, but none seemed ready to come to his defense. The man from the tack shop had retrieved an iron bar, and was approaching Sanjay when a whistle came from afar. A police man rapidly approached, waving his hands in the air.

When he arrived, he helped Sanjay to his feet, while the angry man stood by, shouting more unintelligible words. The police man and the shop owner had an exchange, which Sanjay could not understand, and finally the man turned to head back into his shop. The people started to disperse, and Sanjay was just about to do the same, when the police man seized his arm violently, and started marching him down the road.

Before long, Sanjay found himself locked in a small, but very clean and tidy cell. It was so clean, in fact, that Sanjay imagined he was the first person to have ever used it.

For about an hour, he was simply beside himself with shock. Then, he became angry. He shouted into the prison, but his shouts seemed to reach no one who cared. Finally, as the evening was evidencing itself through his barred window in glorious rays of light, Sanjay slumped into a corner and fell back into that same pensive pondering that he had delved into that very morning as he was plowing his field.

As he pondered, he noticed a flickering in his cell. The flickering became a watery wisp of silver, and then all at once a sort of ill-behaved floating mirror appeared.

Sanjay knew what this meant. He plunged his head into the mirror, eager to be back to where he came from.

Nothing happened. He was still in the jail cell. It was still evening. Sanjay stomped his feet, and was about to throw a glorious tantrum, when he noticed that his cell was considerably dirtier than when he had arrived. In fact, it was filthy. Everything was disgusting. Sanjay looked around, and noticed that the door to the cell was unlocked!

Without wasting a moment, Sanjay made a quiet but hasty escape. No one stopped him. Into the street he ran, and no one stopped him. Down the darkening road he trundled, and no one stopped him. In his retreat Sanjay failed to notice the potholes, mud patches, and peeling paint, a marked difference from the town he had entered. He didn't realize how odd it was that everyone was already inside for the night, so soon after sundown.

After running for a while in the direction he had come from that morning, Sanjay finally slowed to a walk. Perhaps, he thought, he could get home now.

A band of robbers had quite another idea.

Their idea, Sanjay found out, was to hide in the bushes a few miles outside of town, and wait for any late travelers. When they found them, their next idea was to spring out of the bushes and leap upon said travelers, then relieve them of any valuables that might be weighing them down, and make sport out of beating them senseless.

As you might expect, Sanjay found out about their ideas the hard way. When he regained his senses hours later, he was lying by the side of the road, bruised, beaten, and quite alone in the pitch dark of night. His left leg ached, and he thought it might be broken.

Just then, Sanjay heard the clomp of a horse coming down the road. He winced in pain, but could not move. Slowly, a buggy came up beside him. He thought the horse looked familiar.

"Cider? Is that you?"

A man and a woman were seated in the buggy. The lady hopped down, and gasped when she saw Sanjay.

"Oh my! Goodness, are you alright? John, get down here and help me!"

The kind couple lifted Sanjay into the buggy, where he promptly passed out.

Sanjay awoke in the morning, and found himself in a bed that looked like his own.

"It was all a dream," he thought. But when he tried to move, he realized his leg was bound up, and painfully swollen. As he massaged his leg, a man entered the room.

"Ah, you're up then! You gave us quite a scare, stranger. What were you doing out on the road at night?"

Sanjay explained that he was trying to get home after a long, strange day. The man was kind, and listened, and offered to let him stay there until his leg was well enough that he could walk again. Sanjay accepted thankfully.

"I just have one question," the man said as he was about to leave. "How did you know my horse's name?"

***

Weeks passed. Sanjay got better, but had no hope that leaving this place would help him get home again. As soon as he could walk well enough to leave his small room, he found that he had no further to go; this was in fact his house. It was his house, but at the same time it was John and Mary's house. And Cider, who was his horse, was also John and Mary's.

With nowhere to go, Sanjay offered to stay and help John plant the crops. One warm spring morning, as Sanjay was standing out in the young, green field alone, he got to pondering on the complexities of life. No sooner had he started than a mirror began to materialize. He watched eagerly. After it was fully formed, Sanjay all but dived into it.

As he got up and dusted the warm, soft dirt from his clothes, Sanjay heard the neighing of Cider coming from nearby. There he stood just where Sanjay had left him, plow still attached, standing in the middle of a fully plowed and planted field, with plants half grown up already. Cider shook his head up and down, then leaned over and started chewing on a patch of green.

Sanjay heard his wife calling him from his house, and knew it was time to go in.

Long Orbit on Ariane-Dash-M

> "*It means nothing to me. I have no opinion about it, and I don't care.*"
> – **Pablo Picasso in response to the successful Apollo 11 moon landing**

O utpost Ariane-47 MSTAT-12 was positioned in L5. It was the first manned station in the L5 L-point orbit, and the first station captained by a couple—two scientists of interstellar renown. But even more pioneering than all of this was the event that would take place just six months after the intrepid couple first docked. They would become the first to have a child in space.

Sanjay was born on a Tuesday—that is, it was a Tuesday on Earth. On the station (which everyone called "Ariane-Dash-M" for short), they managed their schedule to optimize research output. That's a fancy way of saying that they planned everything around their work. In their time, Sanjay was born in mid-sleep-cycle 3, orbit 47.051.9411 mark 72.116.2715. Babies are often born mid-sleep-cycle, even in space.

His first few years were full of excitement. There had been billions of first smiles on earth, but only one first smile in space; the same was true of first laughs, first tears, first dirty diapers. All of these were epic moments, achievements, milestones. Sanjay, of course, didn't care. He was mesmerized by the stars, and by the knobs on the airlocks, and by pretty much everything. Whether or not it was epic or monumental or scientifically valuable didn't really matter.

When he was six years old (in Earth time), a cargo ship docked with the station, carrying something special. It was a surprise. What you should understand before you hear about this surprise, is that Sanjay's life was mostly about education. He started working on math almost as soon as he could speak. His days were filled with mandated exercises (physical and mental), research, testing, probing, and school. By school, it should be understood that he was homeschooled—or space-station schooled—by his brilliant parents. Sanjay's life was very enjoyable, and very enlivening, but it was also mostly serious.

Things changed on his sixth birthday. Sanjay's parents had a special surprise planned; when the cargo was all unloaded, a case was left in the eleventh node (that's where Sanjay slept). His loving mother excitedly pushed him toward it.

"Decouple the seal, darling." she cooed. "That's the way, rotate clockwise, and don't forget the articulating clasps."

Sanjay lifted the lid slowly. He had never received a birthday present before, not a tangible one. As he peered inside the gray transport case, he saw a fuzzy, pluffy, oddly shaped object. It was roughly humanoid in shape, and had two round plastic disks that approximated eyes. Its ears were misplaced, sticking out of the top of the head, rather than the sides. He didn't know what to think.

"What is it?"

"It's called a Teddy Bear! Give it a hug!"

With some trepidation, Sanjay removed the object. He had hugged his parents, and even some of the crew members, but they usually wrapped him in their arms. It was a new experience to be the larger party, and to wrap this strange new Teddy friend in his arms. He liked it.

"What will you call him?"

Sanjay thought. There was a drink mix that they sometimes had on board, which simulated an earth fruit he had never had; it was called apple cider. It was golden and bright, much like the fur of this new friend.

"I'll call him Cider!"

Soon, the whole station was acquainted with the latest addition to the crew. Sanjay took him everywhere: every class, every exercise, every test. He demanded that Cider be probed as well, to make sure he stayed healthy (the doctors didn't do this, but they pretended to). Sanjay and Cider were inseparable.

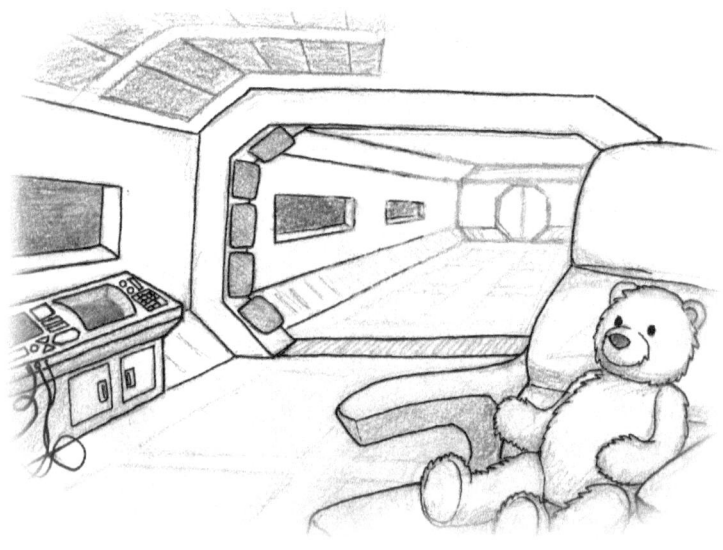

At rest time, when Sanjay was being strapped into his mag-hesive sleeping pod, his mom would place Sanjay in his outstretched arms, then give them both a kiss before floating off to her own node. As soon as the airlock was sealed, the conversation would begin.

"So, what did you learn today, Cider?" Sanjay would ask.

And Cider would tell him.

"I learned more about transfer orbits, and algebra."

"That's good, Cider!"

"And I managed a few radial acceleration equations."

"Very nice! You are learning very quickly. Tomorrow, I will share my sweet rations with you!"

Sometimes, the two would talk late into the sleep-cycle. Sanjay would share what he was learning, and Cider would share what he was picking up. Since neither of them was accustomed to play, this made perfect sense.

Two years passed, and at the age of eight, Sanjay was ready to take on actual crew duties. They were very simple duties, but he was very happy to have them. Cider, however, was given none; Sanjay figured it was because Cider had only been on the station for two years, while he had been on for eight.

"Don't worry, Cider. When you're old like me, you'll be part of the crew too," he would reassure him.

However, Sanjay wasn't so sure. It wasn't that Cider was not capable—he was, in fact, more advanced than Sanjay in several subjects. The problem was that Cider was too shy; he would only talk to Sanjay, and only when no one else was around.

One fractional orbital unit, Sanjay and Cider were on deck as his parents were recording values and running simulations on the station's orbital decay. They were inputting the usual numbers, when his dad had a random impulse.

"Sanjay, you've been studying L5 for a couple years now—what do you think the point stability impact would be if you factor our recent angular adjustments and the cargo dock that came in two kilograms over spec?"

"Viewing the equations theoretically, or taking Trojan bodies into account?"

His father hadn't considered this.

"Well, I'll let you decide—do you know which bodies are close enough to have an effect?"

"I think, last time I checked, Patroclus and Menoetius were non-trivial."

His father looked stunned.

"I hadn't noted that. I'll have to check the data again. Given that then, what do you think on that impact number?"

"Well, let me think."

And Sanjay did think. However, he preferred to think these things through at night, when he could discuss them with Cider. Being put on the spot was not abnormal for him, but as a new crew member, he really, really wanted to get this right.

He had an idea. Moving over to a terminal that was out of sight, he found a bit of privacy and held a council with his trusted friend.

"Cider!" he whispered, "What do you think? I can't be sure of the gravitational force, because I can't recall the mass of Patroclus properly. Do you have any ideas?"

Cider hesitated. He didn't like to speak in front of anyone but Sanjay.

"Cider, please!" Sanjay whispered, even more quietly.

Reluctantly, Cider gave his opinion. His math was solid, and he recalled all the figures. He even considered some things that were out of the ordinary. Sanjay thanked him, and strolled confidently over to his father.

"All things considered," he said, "you should run the simulation with a point stability impact of 0.78551%, and add an angular stability impact of 0.59%. You should adjust your tolerance to plus or minus 0.2—"

Sanjay stopped. He was about to say, "that was Cider's idea," but decided against it.

"Interesting," his father replied.

In a few minutes, the simulation had started, and in a few minutes more time, it had completed.

"What's this!"

It so happened that the simulation terminated in a cataclysmic impact, wherein the station ricocheted off Menoetius, then slammed into Patroclus. At first, Sanjay's father was incredulous. Then, he was concerned. Finally, after re-running the simulation and reviewing the inputs, he became alarmed. So alarmed, in fact, that he opened the clear plastic cover and pressed the big red button marked ALARM, the one that Sanjay had always been curious about.

In short order, the main deck was swarming with crew members, who were busy reviewing numbers and equations and generally working one another into fits. Sanjay and Cider stood by and watched, until his father approached him, along with his mother and two other scientists.

"Sanjay," he said coolly, "I would like you to explain to us how you arrived at the numbers you provided me with."

"Well, I applied the principles you taught me," Sanjay replied, half truthfully.

"Yes, but would you please be more specific?"

"I could try."

And he did try. He reviewed his assumptions, outlined his formulae, and stepped through his results. At times, while the four adults were busy verifying his math, Sanjay consulted quietly with Cider. Eventually, one of scientists noticed Sanjay's whispering, and quietly pointed it out to the two captains.

"Sanjay," his mother said, kneeling, "can we put Cider in his node for now? I think all this might be a bit much for him."

"Oh, I hadn't considered that."

Sanjay thought. He needed Cider, to explain the mathematics that had caused so literal an alarm. Again, he cupped his hand around Cider's ears and whispered.

"Cider! My mom says you might be fatigued. Can you continue to function, just until we solve this problem?"

He held his head close and listened. Cider, though nervous from all the attention, responded.

"Yes. I'm not a crew member, but I feel responsible too. I can continue to help you perform your duties Sanjay."

"He says he's fine," Sanjay announced. His parents looked at one another with an odd sort of look.

"Sanjay," His father inquired, "your approach to the simulation was unique, but we've reviewed it thoroughly and feel that you may have actually discovered a possible scenario; the probabilities are unreasonably high that your simulation is in fact likely."

"Thank you."

"However, there is a piece of the puzzle that we can't quite wrap our heads around. In your point stability and tolerance adjustment—how did you come to the combination? Could you walk us through?"

Sanjay blushed slightly. He decided that it might be time for the full truth.

"Well, I could. But, I don't think I could do it alone. Cider helped me before—would it be okay if he helped again?"

His parents, taken aback, argued ever so slightly over the request. Sanjay figured it was because Cider wasn't a crew member yet, or because he refused to speak to anyone but him. Eventually, they acquiesced. Sanjay, by working through bits, and whispering to Cider for help, walked the stunned scientists through his mathematics.

"That's brilliant!" the chief of operations declared.

"Absolutely breathtaking!" added his mother.

"Genius!" exclaimed the navigational commander, "And Sanjay, how would you suggest we compensate? Have you evaluated the thrust adjustment program? Would you look at our proposed modifications?"

Sanjay's father beamed. Sanjay, however, was uncomfortable.

"Well, Cider did most of it. He is generally ahead of me in our studies."

The adults laughed.

"Well, 'Cider' can certainly help too! Come, have a look!"

He did as he was asked, and with Cider's help, they identified four fatal errors in the navigational corrections. The simulations were run, and the findings confirmed. In the end, Sanjay and Cider successfully averted an utter disaster for the station that had been their only home.

After the ruckus was through, the crew was assembled for a special meal, in honor of Sanjay's accomplishment. Sanjay got double sweets rations, and a liquid packet of apple cider.

As Sanjay shared the treats with his best friend, who was finally warming up to the crew, Cider exclaimed loudly:

"This has been a most fortuitous adventure! To a long orbit on the Ariane-dash-M!"

No one was looking at Cider, and no one noticed where the proclamation had come from, but the whole crew responded:

"To a long orbit on the Ariane-dash-M!"

Rules, Propriety, and Expectations

"Once you see the boundaries of your environment, they are no longer the boundaries of your environment."
– Marshal McLuhan

It was a sweaty, blistery, chafing sort of day. The early summer sun meant it was a great day to be at the market, but the heat meant it wasn't necessarily comfortable. Sanjay was used to it, and would never have issued a complaint based on the weather alone, no matter how bad it got. His complaint, in this case, stemmed from the footfall of a grand horse, whose owner had pushed it a little too far and a little too fast, into the crowded street.

It was Sanjay's foot (as a matter of specificity) that happened to be on the little bit of cobblestone that the horse wished—or was compelled—to use. No damage was done, thankfully, but there was some surprise and some pain—and from Sanjay, some yelling.

All of this happened in an instant, and when the instant was over, Sanjay looked up to see who the rider was. He didn't know her, but he immediately recognized from her horse, its fittings, her clothing, and everything about her, that she was in a lofty station, high above his own. He immediately bowed and apologized for his outburst, but the damage was already done. The now-hushed crowd watched as she dismounted, faced Sanjay, and taught him a public lesson.

In those days, and in that place, a public lesson simply meant a slap on the face. Sanjay knew this, and he tolerated it —though it was wrong, it was the custom, and they both had their roles in the world. However, her slap was followed by a tirade, and another slap. This was more than was due, and it hurt his pride. Still, when someone of her station strayed from their place there was no punishment, and so Sanjay went on with his day, and forgot about the incident as soon as his foot stopped aching.

Sanjay, though lowly, was a great man in his own way. He was the most respected animal trainer and healer within a thousand miles, and his services were always in high demand. His station regulated his pay, and so his talents weren't allowed to go to his head—but nevertheless, he was a great man, who served all the greatest men of the highest stations. At least those within a thousand miles.

A week after his encounter at the market (and, really, only about five or six days after his foot stopped hurting), Sanjay received a summons to appear at the Brighton Estate. Nicholas Brighton was the richest landowner that anyone had ever heard of, and so you might fancy that Sanjay was nervous; however, he had been summoned to many rich-last-name estates, and he knew exactly what it meant. It meant that they had work for him to do. It meant that he would be able to provide more food and clothing for his aging parents and younger siblings.

The Brighton Estate, he noticed as he walked down the avenue leading to the main buildings, was particularly grand. It had sweeping lawns, an old arching tree canopy, and imposing stables that made Sanjay's heart ache. When he arrived, he was called into the house, and led into a sitting room, where Nicholas was waiting for him.

"Come in! Come in, young man! I have heard many, many good and wonderful stories about you!"

Sanjay entered sheepishly, stood in front of the man, and bowed.

"Not like that! Come, sit!"

Though not used to being asked to sit in a sitting room, Sanjay complied.

Nicholas continued jovially.

"Now, Sanjay—it is Sanjay, right?"

"Yes sir."

"Good. Sanjay, I have a problem. My daughter had a very serious riding accident recently. She is bad enough off, but we have hopes that she will recover. Her horse, on the other hand —well, our stablemen tell me that he must be put down."

Sanjay shuddered. All too often, this was the proposed solution, especially from rich, lazy stablemen.

"I'm not so sure, and I'd like a second opinion—a solid, experienced opinion."

Sanjay rose to his feet. Nicholas laughed, and motioned for him to sit back down.

"You see, Sanjay, this is my daughter's favorite horse. He's a beast of a thing, unruly and headstrong—just like her, actually! But, he didn't come cheap; I brought that horse here myself, as a gift. I thought he might calm my daughter down a bit with his spirit!"

Nicholas leaned in. Sanjay leaned back a little.

"I'll tell you what I'm going to do, Sanjay. I'll make it worth your while, double your usual pay, if you can help me out here. If by your craft you can heal Cider—that's the horse's name, you see—I'll pay you double your fee."

Sanjay had heard about these kinds of offers, but had never had one, and it made him uneasy. He started to protest.

"But, sir, it's not usual—"

"No, no, I insist. I don't care about custom! I've been around long enough, and visited enough places, to know that when you want something—really want something—you throw custom and caution to the wind! I won't speak to anyone about our arrangement, and I'm sure you won't. And, I'll pay you myself when the time comes."

Sanjay thought. He could certainly use the money, and men of rich-last-name estates never went back on their word. The deciding factor was the simple reality that he honestly didn't know how to say no to someone of Nicholas' station, having never made the attempt.

"Yes sir, I will do as you ask. But, I will need to look at the horse first, to give you an idea of whether or not your stablemen are correct."

The two shook hands on the agreement, then went immediately to the stables. The horse was badly off. Sanjay spent a full thirty minutes examining him from every angle. At first it looked like there was no hope, but after close examination Sanjay determined that there were in fact no broken bones, only strained muscles and deep unseen wounds.

"It will take time, sir, but I believe I can heal this horse."

"Exceptional!"

Nicholas came close, and Sanjay almost thought the strange man would try to hug him, but he only clasped his shoulders and shook his hand.

"You'll start right away then?"

"Yes sir. I will need to walk back to town, to get some special supplies—"

Before he could finish the sentence, Nicholas put his fingers to his lips and let out a piercing whistle. A footman appeared, and was ordered to take Sanjay anywhere he needed to go, and supply him with any purchases he required, immediately.

As he rode in the carriage (for the first time in his life!), Sanjay thought about his curious fortune. This Nicholas Brighton was a good man, not just a rich man, and he determined he would do everything he could for him.

Cider, it turned out, had thrown his rider as he was pushed at full speed near the edge of a steep ravine. As one hoof slipped, the clever horse saw what was coming, and bucked just in time. The girl was thrown into a tree, and then landed on some rocks quite hard indeed, but avoided tumbling down the precipice with the massive horse, which surely would have killed her. It took two carts, four horses, and twenty men to pull the horse out.

The injuries were great. On the first day, Sanjay spent the entire afternoon and evening cleaning and dressing wounds properly, with a special salve that he had invented for the treatment of such wounds on horses. He continued to work into the night, making sure the horse's stalls were filled with clean straw, and instructing the stable master (who was also a good man, and who had been told to give Sanjay anything he asked for) on the number of men that would be required to move the horse regularly, to avoid putting too much pressure on any one part of the horse's body from lying too long in one position. Finally, before leaving late that night, he sat and massaged Cider's aching muscles while he sang to him of meadows and fields, clouds and streams.

Perhaps these methods sound strange to you and me, but to a master trainer and healer, they are essential tools. Medicine, massage, and music are three ancient and powerful forces.

For several days this continued. Because his client was insistent, Sanjay spared no expense. Cider had the best herbs and ointments, the best stalls and freshest grasses, and the most attention that Sanjay had ever been able to give to one animal.

In two weeks, Cider was back on his feet. Normally, animal owners would take an animal that was healed to this condition, and manage the rest of the process with their own stablemen, to save money and to have the lowly Sanjay off their property. But not Nicholas.

"Sanjay!" he cried out, as he approached the stables after hearing that Cider was doing better.

"Yes sir. We're over here."

Sanjay was walking Cider slowly across the lawn, in the warm sun.

"Sanjay, I'm glad I caught you. My footman said that you had ordered the carriage to get some medicine for the stable storehouse, and that you were planning to go home!"

"Yes sir. Cider is well enough now, your men can take over from here."

Nicholas frowned. Even in his frown he looked like he was secretly smiling.

"You know more about this than I do, Sanjay, but I would really rather have you working with Cider, until he is completely restored. No expense is too great—must I sweeten the deal?"

Sanjay had never heard of this, except in fantastic stories. Of course, he at least knew that he must refuse.

"No sir, you are very kind already. If you wish it, I will stay."

"Good! You see, my daughter never properly trained this horse. I fear it is too much for her. When Cider is well, I am hopeful that you can help with that too. I hear you are quite capable."

"If you wish it, sir."

Nicholas clapped him on the shoulder.

"So modest! I do wish it. And, I wish you would stop calling me 'sir'. That's what I always had to call my father, and it never feels quite right when people call me that. Call me Nicholas."

Sanjay's mouth fell open. Nicholas noticed, and laughed.

"Oh my! I'm sorry, my boy, I forget all the blasted customs sometimes, they mean so little to me! If you can't do that, please just call me Mr. Brighton, that will do nicely."

He practiced saying "Mr. Brighton" in his head all afternoon, so he could get used to the notion. Sanjay was thrilled that he had been asked to stay on. He had grown quite fond of Cider, and he wanted to ensure a full and complete recovery.

It was around this time that Sanjay was informed that Miss Constance Brighton, Nicholas' daughter, wished to be brought to see the horse. She, herself, was still healing, and would be brought to the stables in what they called a "Bath Chair"—a sort of lounge chair with wheels.

Sanjay imagined that with such a fine father, Miss Brighton would be such a fine girl. However, before she arrived, he could hear her yelling at her servants from across the lawns, and he started to imagine that perhaps she was more like many other daughters of rich-last-name estates that he had encountered in the past. He decided that he would wait in the stable with Cider until she called for him.

When she called, he brought the horse out to greet her, using its large body to shield him from view. Though he was hiding behind Cider, he could hear her gasp audibly at the sight of the horse, then fall silent for a few moments. As he was profoundly educated in the subtle movements of the finest horses, Sanjay knew without seeing when Miss Brighton's hand caressed Cider's leg.

"Come 'round, boy, so I can see you."

Sanjay walked around and bowed to greet the young woman. As he rose, he recognized her immediately as the girl from the market, the one who had offered a greater punishment than was customary. For a moment she looked at him, trying to place his face—then, comprehension, and she looked away uncomfortably.

"He is doing rather better than I thought possible. My stablemen told me he was as good as dead after they dragged him out of the ditch. What did you do, then?"

Sanjay explained, and she listened thoughtfully. When he was done, she sat quietly for a moment, then ordered her servants to take her back to the house. She did not say goodbye.

The following day, as Sanjay was getting ready to massage and sing to Cider, he heard a commotion, and looked to see what was going on. Miss Brighton, with her entourage, was again approaching the stables. When she arrived, he looked at her inquiringly.

"I've come," she announced, "to watch."

He wasn't used to an audience, but didn't know how to say no to someone in Miss Constance Brighton's station, so he collected himself and began his work. He massaged Cider's legs while he sang a peaceful song about a river that he knew as a very small child. The song spoke of the gentlest flowing waters, the most quiet inlet brooks, and the shade of unspeakably steady trees. The miss never said a word, she only sighed from time to time.

Miss Brighton's visits continued for three days, before she spoke again.

"Boy, I want you to do to my legs what you're doing to Cider's."

Sanjay started, and the servants gasped. In their views, the request was impertinent, inappropriate, and impossible. Sanjay knew this. The servants knew this.

Sanjay didn't know what to say. The servants just looked at one another, in shock. Finally, Miss Brighton spoke again.

"What?! To the deuce with customs and rules and propriety! My own doctors have told me that I may never walk again, does that mean nothing? Never ride again! My horse—my precious Cider—was near death, and you brought him back. You made him walk again! I demand that you treat me as well!"

Sanjay looked at the servants, but they were just as lost as he was.

"Please?"

Her tone was soft, pleading. In a moment, his heart melted, and Sanjay forgot about customs. He forgot about rules, and propriety, and expectations. And, he forgot about punishments, the severe type that might come if Mr. Nicholas Brighton saw that he was massaging his daughter's leg the way he massaged Cider's. None of this mattered. Only healing mattered.

"Come, let me look."

The servants were aghast, but said nothing to her as they wheeled her close. After a few minutes of poking and prodding, Sanjay made a determination.

"Your legs are weakened from disuse, Miss, but they are not beyond healing. If you come here every day, I will do what I can."

Miss Brighton let out a gasp, then covered her eyes. She was crying.

"Now, mind you, I think we should ask Mr. Brighton—"

"No!"

Her hands dropped, and her hot tears turned once again to an anger which she had not yet learned to control.

"I do not need my father's permission! You all," she said, turning to her servants, "will say nothing to my father, and you'll not speak of this in your late-night gossip, or so help me!"

"You," she commanded, turning to me, "will start today."

Sanjay, who had still not figured out how to say no to someone of Miss Brighton's station, obeyed. While he sang, he massaged Miss Brighton's legs. This continued every day; he would work on Cider, and he would work on Miss Brighton, and both would improve.

After a while, Miss Brighton was standing. After a while longer, she was walking, and finally, she stopped coming to the stables. It was only a few days after she stopped that Nicholas came down.

"Sanjay!" he said in his usual cheery manner, "I have heard such tales of your progress, that I had to come and see for myself!"

And he did see; Cider was fully restored. Sanjay took him out on the field, and demonstrated a walk, a trot, a gallop, and even a jump. His golden-apple coat, which he was named for, glistened in the sun, and very little remained in the way of scars. In all respects, he was the strong, healthy horse that he had been before the accident. In some respects, he was even better.

"It is indeed a miracle! You have earned your wages, Sanjay, and I am happy to pay them!" Mr. Nicholas paid Sanjay on the spot, double his usual rates, just as he had promised. No one was there to witness, or to complain about this graciousness.

"Now, Sanjay, I have something else to talk to you about. Will you walk with me?"

Sanjay hadn't ever taken a stroll with a great man, but he didn't know how to refuse, so he tied up Cider and the two began their walk. For a while, they walked in silence. Nicolas eventually started to speak.

"I have to tell you something. My daughter, when you came, was very bad off. I had hope still, but that hope started to fade. Then, miraculously, she started to get better."

Sanjay felt an uncomfortable knot in his stomach, the kind that you feel when you're keeping something inside that you know you shouldn't hide.

Nicholas continued.

"Now she is well enough—and Cider is too—that I think she could start riding again. But, she is still as headstrong as ever, and I worry that if she and Cider don't get some correction in their way of seeing things, they'll end up over a cliff."

"Yes, Mr. Brighton."

He smiled, and clapped Sanjay on the shoulder.

"I like you! A man of very few words, but when you do speak, it's to the point! 'Yes, Mr. Brighton' indeed. So, you agree with me. Now, my view of the thing is that they both need to be trained. You'd be too humble to say it, but I've heard from more than one of my friends that you are the best trainer in a thousand miles—don't try to deny it or downplay it, I have it on authority! I want you to train Cider to be a world-class riding horse—and I want you to do it with Constance on his back. I know you've been here quite some time, and I'm prepared to make it worth your while—"

Sanjay, uncharacteristically, interrupted before Nicholas could "sweeten the deal."

"Yes, Mr. Brighton, I would be more than happy to train Cider, and to teach Miss Brighton, for my usual rate."

Nicholas smiled widely, and the deal was made. The next day, Nicholas and his daughter appeared at the stables together.

"Sanjay, I've informed my daughter that you will be re-training Cider. After so long in recovery, it will be like a fresh start for him. Miss Constance Brighton—"

At her name, he motioned for her to come forward. They were being formally introduced, something that had never happened to Sanjay.

"Miss Constance Brighton, I would like you to meet Sanjay; Sanjay, my daughter Miss Constance Brighton."

He waited while Sanjay and Constance looked at one another uncomfortably. They had seen each other every day for more than a month, but must now pretend to have never met. And, there was the question of stations—this formal introduction was out of sorts, and they both knew it.

"Come now, shake hands! There, that's the spirit. You two will be working closely together, it is proper in my book that you be introduced. Now, Constance, I say this in front of

Sanjay so that you know your place—Sanjay is your teacher, and you are his student. He is known as the best healer and trainer for a thousand miles, you would do well to mind him."

Constance looked down at the ground.

"Yes, I know."

"Sanjay, I don't have to explain to you that I'm taking some great liberties in the way I'm doing things here. I may not think much of customs, but I know them well enough to know that I'm stepping all over them, and I know you understand what I mean. I trust you, Sanjay. That is all I will say, and I'll leave it at that."

The familiar knot was coming back to Sanjay's stomach, but he just swallowed hard and nodded.

Summer was fading when Sanjay started training Constance and Cider. They were just as headstrong as Nicholas had said, but Sanjay was patient and wise and kind. Fall arrived in its splendor, and through the gold and red leaves Cider and Constance bounded with confidence. Stubbornness and pride faded, and an excitement and willingness to learn replaced them. Both students were eager, and with that a good teacher can do anything. Soon, they were as accomplished as any horse and rider that Sanjay had ever worked with.

Something inside Sanjay changed too, over the course of his stay at the Brighton Estate. Whereas he had once considered himself lowly, he had grown to see that he was worthy of respect. Whereas he once stooped, he now stood tall. And a consideration entered his being that he hadn't previously known: Love. He knew that he loved Mr. Nicholas Brighton, as a kind and caring man who didn't look only at your station, but considered your character. But he also faintly knew that he loved Cider, the most beautiful horse he had ever seen; and that he loved Miss Constance Brighton, the most beautiful young lady that had ever walked the earth.

In the deepest part of fall the time for training was completed. Mr. Brighton had ordered a show of Cider and Constance's progress, for all the household to watch. Tables were laid out on the lawns, with a bounteous fall feast, and a course was setup in the grass. Sanjay, who stood with Mr. Brighton, watched with a keen pleasure as Constance made every turn and every jump with grace and precision.

When they finished and returned, Sanjay held out his hand to help Constance down, and as her feet touched the ground, a tear streamed down his face. As she alighted, he kept holding her hand. She looked at him and curtsied, but still he held her hand. He knew this would be the last time he saw her, the last time he touched her soft skin as she got down from her ride. He knew that all were watching them—that Mr. Brighton was watching them—and he knew he had to let go, but he could not.

"I have to tell you something, Mr. Brighton."

He spoke to Mr. Brighton, but he was looking Constance in the eyes, and still clasping her hand.

"I have to tell you, or it will eat me up inside. You can do as you wish with me—do anything to me—and I won't complain, but I can't be untrue to you. You have been too kind.

"After you asked me to stay, until Cider was healed, Miss Brighton came to me. She just wanted to check on Cider. I didn't stop her, I didn't turn her away for impropriety. It was not her fault, it was not her servant's fault, it was mine.

"That day, she asked me to heal her, the way I healed Cider."

Several servants gasped audibly. Constance pulled her hand away and covered her mouth. Sanjay turned to face Nicholas.

"I am an honest man, Mr. Brighton, and I know my place. But when she said 'Please', something inside me just snapped, and I forgot all of that. I forgot what you might do, and I forgot what it might mean to you and to her and to everyone. I only saw someone that was broken, and I saw that I could heal her. And, sir, I did. I did heal her, just the way I healed Cider."

A complete silence had fallen on the dinner party. Only the blowing leaves and birds dared make a sound. Sanjay, having finished his confession, hung his head low. The seconds seemed endless. Finally, Mr. Nicholas Brighton reached over and lifted Sanjay's chin. Sanjay closed his eyes and prepared for the hardest blow he would ever receive in his life—and possibly the last. But it never came. Eventually, he opened his eyes. Nicholas was smiling at him.

"Thank you for telling me, Sanjay."

Sanjay was swept away by a wave of relief, and tears began streaming down his face. This man, who could have killed him for his actions, was thanking him.

Nicholas spoke loudly, so all could hear.

"When Constance started improving, I began to watch her more closely to find out what was making a difference, so that I could encourage it. I had lost hope, and scarcely dared to believe. But, when I saw that she was going to Sanjay, everything changed. Somehow I knew that she would be all right."

"You mean," Sanjay asked, "that you knew, and you still asked me to train Cider and teach Miss Brighton?"

"Yes, I knew. I knew that you had succeeded in healing them both in body, and I felt that you might be able to heal them both in spirit."

Sanjay didn't know what to think.

"You see, Sanjay, ever since you came here, you've demonstrated that you know your place. You've shown that you believe in your station. I don't blame you, it's what you've been taught. But, I've been taught something entirely different.

"I learned on the battlefield, that it doesn't matter what your station is. Men of my own station, but of another country, had managed to place a ball through one of my arms and a knife through one of my legs. There I lay, ready to die, when a man of your station came to my aid. He was a cook in our camp, and watching from afar he saw that we were losing the battle. He ran through the thick of it to get to my side, and no one paid him any heed because of his station. He dragged me off that field, and no one paid him any heed because of his station. We hid in the jungle for I don't know how long, and he nursed me back to health. He found herbs and packed them into my wounds. He tore up his own cloths and made bandages. He fed me, and nourished me. One day he covered me with leaves when a patrol was coming, and then went and drew them off. I heard two shots, and never saw my friend again."

"This man was a hero, Sanjay. He was noble, brave, and full of love. When I look at you, with your gifts and talents and humility, I see him."

Nicholas pulled Sanjay in and hugged him tightly for several long moments. The servants, unable to hold back, were sniffling, and Constance was crying quietly.

"After the lovely performance today, I know you've helped my daughter more than anyone else ever could have. I haven't seen her this happy since we lost her mother. Perhaps you think you are one thing, Sanjay, but I think you are another. Perhaps my servants have their ideas, but I have mine, and I am in charge. This is my house, my household, and my family.

"Of course, I don't speak for everyone..."

He looked at Constance.

"But, for my part, I wish for you to stay. You can have a permanent place working in the stables if you like, but you won't be a servant, you'll be a guest. And, let it grow from there however it will—as for me, I bless it all."

Sanjay stood silently. Looking at this great man, he felt that he grasped his meaning, and his heart leaped. He glanced at Constance. She smiled, and held out her hand. Blissfully, he took it in his once more.

A Healer at the Bywater Inn

"There are two kinds of charlatan: the man who is called a charlatan, and the man who really is one. The first is the quack who cures you; the second is the highly qualified person who doesn't."
– G. K. Chesterton

Every village has a personality. Camdenville for example is angry, impatient, and cynical. In Camdenville, an enraged mob will tie your foot to the back of a wagon and drag you out of town, just for looking at the bartender the wrong way. If the weather is bad, they might do it for no reason at all.

So, when Sanjay strolled into the Darkmire Tavern on a dreary, rainy Monday afternoon, there was already an excellent chance that things would end poorly. He knew this, however, and came prepared.

"Gentleman!" he called out, as three burly and sour-faced men rose and started toward him. "I'm looking for a knife-maker with uncommon skill. Behold these bones—"

The men paused as Sanjay drew twelve small white bones from a pouch, and rattled them in his hand.

"These are the right-hand finger-bones of a witch who died from the plague—"

There was an audible gasp, and the rough and sharp sound of chairs being hastily scooted away from him at every table. He saw several men searching for something to throw.

"Have no fear, my friends, there's no risk of disease. This witch died more than a year ago, a thousand miles from this spot. I've carried these bones all this way, without any harm. In fact, I'd say that my luck has been rather better than usual. Why, just two days hence, a man lifted his arm to strike me, and he fell dead where he stood—dead, just like that!"

Sanjay snapped his fingers. A small whimper came from a dark corner, and the men's eyes widened.

"No, I'm not here to make anyone uncomfortable, I just need a knife maker. You see, I need to carve these bones, to make them more useful, and I need a very specific knife to do it with. Before she died, this witch told me exactly how to do it—"

"Alright, stranger," came the wavering voice of the bartender. "You've no business in here, and we're in no right mood to hear any more. The knife maker goes by the name of Calvin, and his shop is at the south edge of town. It's the house with the tall gate posts."

Satisfied that he had made the impression he intended to make, Sanjay tipped his hat and walked out.

Now, Sanjay already knew where the knife maker lived. He also knew that half the men in that tavern were travelers passing through on their way to Dale, a town that was cynical without being impatient or angry. He indeed wanted a knife, and he really was going to carve the small bones in his pouch, but more than anything else, he was keen on making an impression.

After buying the knife, he made a show of carving the bones very slowly, as he sat by the roadside in the rain. A few of the men from the tavern, filled with curiosity, followed him at a distance and watched. He carved through the evening, and at nightfall he carved still. In the morning some men from the tavern came to the spot and found him patiently scraping and whittling away. Stopping only to eat and drink from the supplies he carried, Sanjay took the better part of two days carving those bones. When he was done, he packed up and started off into the woods.

***

It was a rainy Monday morning (that same rainy Monday we just talked about, but earlier in the day) when Cider rode into Camdenville behind a band of traveling farm hands. He soon learned that they, like he, were stopping only for a rest on their way to Dale ("for where better to spend all that one has earned, than in the cool shades and calm waters of Dale?" as the expression goes). Cider, with his wild frock of bright red hair and arms that were as big as small tree trunks (and just as hard), made friends with the laborers quickly. Just one look at him and no one wanted to dislike him, for fear of what he might be capable of.

The new friends sat, ate, and drank together as they took their break in Camdenville. Cider was the most gregarious of the bunch, sharing every small detail of his past work season with them. By mid-afternoon, the lot were fast friends, determined to wend their way to Dale as a group.

They were finishing up one last round of drinks—Cider was buying!—when Sanjay walked in with his discomforting bones. Cider, being the largest of the bunch he was with, set the tone. His chair slid back in horror at the mention of the plague, so their chairs slid back. When others grabbed at bottles to throw, he grabbed at an entire table. When Sanjay left the Darkmire, Cider said to the group:

"Friends, I don't know what you think of the man, but to me he looks like trouble. I don't know a thing about carving bones, but if I see that man again, It'll be the bones in his body, not the bones in his leather pouch, that he'll be worrying about!"

All heartily agreed, and with that they set off together for Dale.

***

It was Wednesday morning when Sanjay gently placed the finished finger-bones into his pouch and started his journey toward Dale. It wasn't until Thursday evening that he pushed open the door of the Bywater Inn. Many of the travelers he had seen in the Darkmire at Camdenville were already there, and some recognized him. Certainly, the same ill feelings existed toward the strange plague-bone-carving fellow; however, it had been exactly twelve years, four months, and twenty-three days since anyone had been dragged out of Dale behind a wagon, and that had been for a very good reason. The sorts of mischief that were tolerated in Camdenville were not generally tolerated here in Dale, so the uncomfortable patrons held their peace.

Sanjay strolled up to the bar and took a seat next to a massive, red-haired man. As he called to the bartender for a draft, the man turned and recognized him.

"You!" Cider roared, turning to Sanjay.

The noise of the room died all at once. In the quiet, you could hear clearly as the men who had been traveling with Cider whispered, "it's the man with the bones!"

"Can I help you?" Sanjay said innocently.

"You can walk out that door, with me right behind you! Then, in the open, I can help you—help you fly through the air and into a tree!"

Cider stood up suddenly and violently, knocking his stool to the ground. His friends looked at one another, but sat frozen in their spots.

"Oh, it's you!" Sanjay said calmly. Cider took a step closer and snorted in his face.

"Me!? You don't know me!"

"But I do."

"You don't!"

"Just this morning, as I was on the road, I took a break, and consulted these bones that I carry."

Sanjay jiggled the bag at his hip. The men that had been in Camdenville shuddered.

"They told me that I'd meet you. They told me that you'd be large—though I confess, you're rather larger than I thought you would be—and that you would have a problem that only I could help with."

"What!?" billowed Cider. "You, help me? I'll help you, right out of town!"

"They said," Sanjay continued, "that you suffer nightly with a soreness in your left thigh."

The friends that Cider picked up in Camdenville, and who had been with him for the last few days, gasped and started talking in bursts.

"That's right! He told us about that!"

"By Jove, didn't he mention that while we were traveling?"

"Yes, we stopped at a creek to fill our jugs and he was rubbing his leg. I asked him what was wrong, and he said—"

"—that it was an old injury, from three seasons ago?" interrupted Sanjay.

"Exactly! That's what he said exactly!"

"And don't forget," chimed in another, "that Cider said that he doesn't usually talk about it. This man's an oracle!"

Cider lifted his hand and the chatter ceased. He eyed Sanjay up and down.

"So... you've been following us, and spying on our conversations, is that it?"

From another part of the bar, a voice spoke up.

"I watched him carve those—those things, in the rain. He was still carving them when I left Wednesday morning."

"And, he was on foot," one of Cider's friends offered.

"I don't care!" shouted Cider. "However you came to know about my leg, it matters little. When I'm through with you, you won't even remember your own mother's name."

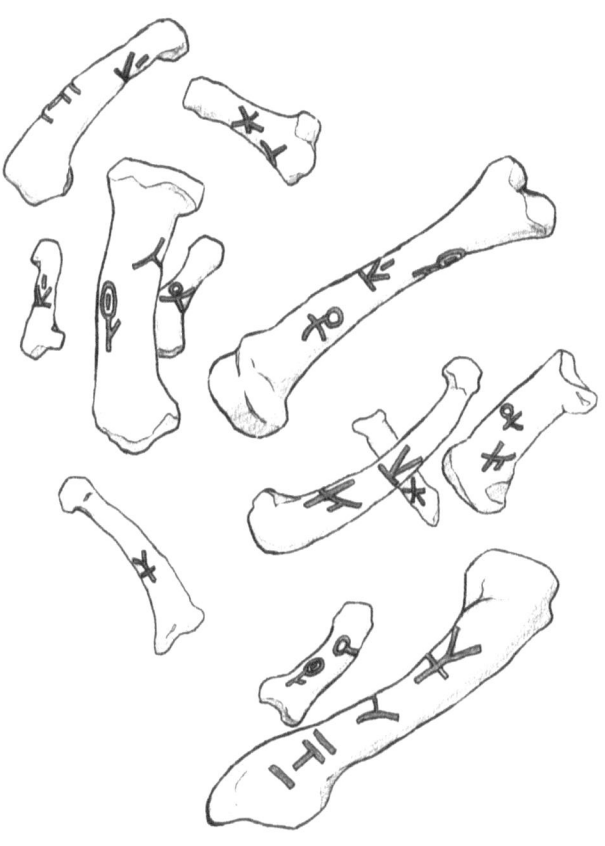

"Ah, but the bones told me how to heal that leg of yours," continued Sanjay. "And, if you work me over as badly as all that, I don't think I'll be able to do it."

At this, Cider paused. One of his friends ventured a thought.

"Well, what if he's right? What could it hurt to find out, before you pummel him?"

"Enough! Tell me, collector of bones, what good you think you can do for me."

"It's a simple enough process. And, we can step outside and take care of business there. Then, if you're not satisfied, you can send me hurtling through the air into the nearest tree. Is it a deal?"

"Deal?!" Cider roared. "A deal implies that we will both get something out of the bargain!"

"Of course," answered Sanjay. "If it works, I assume that you'll pay me for my services, naturally."

Cider drew his fist back, but Sanjay continued hurriedly.

"Never fear, never fear. If it doesn't work, you'll pay nothing. If it does, I leave it up to you whether you feel it's fair to pay or not. You're large enough, I can hardly bargain for more..."

Cider thought for a few moments, his fist still drawn back as if to strike. Finally, his arm dropped as he decided.

"Very well. We take this outside. My friends will come with us, in case you're the slippery type. We'll hear you out on this 'cure', and if it's reasonable, we'll try it out. If it works, fine. If not—"

Cider made a gesture with his hand, of a person flying through the air, ending with a fist hitting hard on the open palm of his opposite hand.

The lot shuffled their way out to the front of the Bywater Inn. Most of the occupants followed. More collected from the road. Soon, Sanjay and Cider stood in the middle of a large circle of people.

"Well," Cider said, clenching and unclenching his fists. "What's this cure then?"

"I saw it in the bones," explained Sanjay, "but it was a bit complex in the particulars. Do you mind if I consult them again, to make sure that I do it right?"

Cider only nodded.

Sanjay pulled the bones out of his pouch and sat on the ground. He tossed them gently while muttering to himself, then examined them fixedly for some time. Cider's friends whispered to the curious onlookers about the origins of the bones, and the impression he had made in Camdenville.

Finally, Sanjay scooped up the bones, returned them to the pouch, and stood.

"I have it. But I'll need a few herbs. They're common roadside plants, can someone fetch them for us?"

Cider pointed to two of his friends. Sanjay rattled off the names of some weeds, and the two took off.

"Now, if you'll just sit here for a moment..."

Cider sat. Sanjay prodded his leg. He lifted it by the ankle, and let it drop gently to the ground. He picked up two stones, and tapped on the muscles gently.

"Yes, this will certainly work, it's just as I saw."

Soon, the two men returned with the weeds. Sanjay rubbed them together in his hands for a few minutes, and asked Cider to roll up his pant leg. Then, he smeared the plants on Cider's leg while chanting softly, paused, and smacked his leg as hard as he could.

"There! It is done! Stand up and try it out."

Cider did not look amused, but he rose slowly to his feet. He shifted his weight gingerly between his two legs. He rocked back and forth. He walked around the circle of people slowly. He jumped up and down.

"By Zeus, I think it does feel better!"

With those words he sprinted around the circle, and jumped up as high as he could, landing hard on both legs.

"It feels better than it has in years! The pain is gone!"

Cider hooped and hollered, rolled on the ground and sprang up, leaped around clapping all the onlookers on the back any time he came close enough.

"It's a miracle!"

With that, he ran over to Sanjay, and scooped him into the air. Instead of throwing him into the nearest tree trunk, he gave him a huge oak-armed hug.

Word went out, "There's a healer at the Bywater Inn!", and Sanjay was the center of attention in Dale for the rest of the day. Not only did Cider pay him generously, others lined up for hours, practically throwing their money at Sanjay to have a consultation with the bones. Sanjay recommended cures and gave out recipes, while the towns people filled his bag with gold. At the end of the night, after everyone had gone home, Sanjay slipped quietly out of town. Cider too, checked out of the inn, and started a new voyage.

***

Neither Camdenville nor Dale ever laid eyes on Sanjay or Cider again. But the two met up the very next day, at a secret location deep in the woods near the spring that feeds Coal Creek. They had met there weeks prior, to plan the particulars of their little escapade in Dale. The story of the hurt leg, the timing of the travel between the two towns, the friends Cider would have to make; nothing was left to chance. They'd spend the next year traveling to a distant country, and coming up with a new plan to part more fools from their money. It wasn't an honest living, but it was the life they lived, at least this time around.

Llama Guard Duty

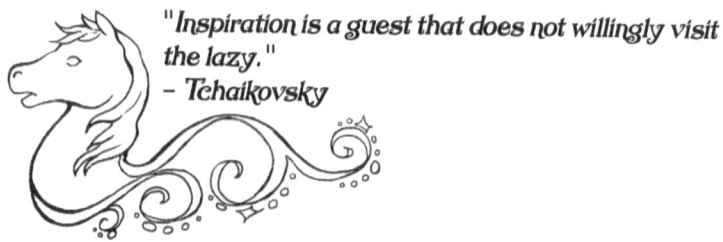

"Inspiration is a guest that does not willingly visit the lazy."
– Tchaikovsky

Sanjay loved guard days. On such days he would volunteer for three consecutive daytime watches, strap the pillion on his tiger, Cider, and together they'd trot out along the patrol paths until about noon. In the glade near Dalton's rock, he would snack on Guanabana that were so ripe you could bring them down just by shaking the tree, then sit in the shade and sip Huito juice from the gourd he carried at his hip. When he had his fill, he'd turn Cider loose to watch him chase Capybara.

Nothing ever happened on patrol days. At least, nothing hard. No one dared attack the Tamaldali tribe, who were known throughout the valley for two things: their amazing crops, and their formidable tiger-mounted warriors.

This, unfortunately, was not a patrol day. This was a supply day. Nothing easy ever happened on supply days. On this particular supply day, Sanjay had been tasked with leading a small group of pack llamas by the banks of the river to harvest Terra Preta, the rich soil that his tribe depended on for growing an impressive variety of foods. It was back-breaking work, and messy to boot. After what felt like endless hours in the baking-hot sun, Sanjay had six llamas laden with baskets full of dirt, and a back that throbbed like it was about to fall off.

Cider, on the other hand, had been relaxing in the shade. He had caught his fill of Capybara, spent an hour cleaning his coat, slept, and generally behaved the way you'd expect a gigantic domesticated cat to behave. When Sanjay clicked his tongue for Cider to come, he did so only after stretching and yawning expansively.

"You lazy cat. You've done nothing but play all day long, while I've been hard at work loading up these llamas!"

Cider, pretending not to understand, leaned down and licked his paw.

"I have a mind to let you lead them back on your own, while I rest in the shade! I do! What would you say to that?"

Still playing the fool, Cider looked at him sideways.

Sanjay thought.

"Say, these llama's know their way home, and they know that when they get there these baskets will be removed and they'll be fed. They're dying to get home! Why, I bet if we got them started, they'd make it the rest of the way on their own. What do you think about that?"

Cider thought it was a foolish idea, but he didn't say anything. Sanjay was always scheming up new ways to avoid his work, and Cider didn't think it was right. Even though he enjoyed lounging about like any self-respecting tiger would, he didn't really think it was becoming of a human, and especially not a warrior in the Tamaldali Guard—even if Sanjay was the youngest of the group.

Sanjay, pleased at his cleverness, started to mount up Cider's pillion as he continued to scheme.

"Oh man, this will be great! We'll get them going, and follow behind. At the fork in the path, the one near old Dolo's place, we'll split off and leave them to walk the rest of the way alone. Then we can go and see if the Pitahaya are ripe."

The path was easy, the llamas were focused on their burden, and soon Sanjay and Cider found themselves at the edge of the Pitahaya grove just as Sanjay had schemed. The spiky, wiggly, other-worldly plants were laden with fruit. Cider wasn't fond of fruit, and he was still full of Capybara, so he calmly walked the rows as Sanjay squeezed the plump red produce in search of his prize.

Sanjay, hungrier than usual, took a while to fill his belly. By the time he was done, the light had dropped low enough that the shadows from the villainous Pitahaya plants were slithering snake-like on the soft brown dirt of the grove. He clicked his tongue in the way that meant, "let's go home," and the two set off without a word.

They doubled-back to the fork in the road, and found Dolo standing there waiting.

"Sanjay! Come! Come here quick!"

Obediently, Sanjay stopped Cider near the old man.

"I'm so glad you've come! I'm old, and can't manage on my own, but when I heard the angry trill of a llama in trouble, I grabbed my cane and—"

"Llama in trouble!"

Sanjay didn't have to hear more. If those llama's didn't make it back, there would be consequences in the form of triple supply duty—or worse. He tapped Cider's haunch with his heel, and the two set off before old Dolo could finish his sentence.

A few minutes down the trail, Sanjay saw a dark heap of freshly dug earth. One of the llama's had dropped a part of their load of Terra Preta near an embankment.

"Oh no!" Sanjay cried out, "what if one of them tumbled down into that ravine! We need to check!"

With a tug and a tap of the heel, he directed Cider to the edge. In his haste, he pushed a little too hard, and got the pair a little too close a little too quickly. Cider, being rather clever, and rather averse to tumbling into ravines, brought them to a skidding halt just in time.

"Whoa boy! Whoa! That was close, we almost—"

As he was expressing his relief, Sanjay leaned forward to determine how deep the ravine really was. In an instant their weight shifted just enough to break the dirt they were standing on loose, and the startled pair toppled over the edge.

Cats might topple gracefully on their own, but with Tamaldali guard soldiers clutching pillions on their backs, things are different. In a chaotic and confused jumble of skin and fir, the two flipped, flopped, dropped, and plummeted heads-and-tails into the depths of the ravine.

They eventually came to a halt, but it took another several minutes for their heads to stop spinning.

"Cider! Are you all right?"

Sanjay got up and staggered over to his friend. Cider was fine physically, but his massive feline ego was considerably bruised. He turned his head away defiantly.

"Oh, come now," Sanjay crooned as he checked him over, "you don't look that bad. That was some fall though!"

He looked up, and drew a sharp breath of astonishment.

"That's impossible!"

The ravine edge—the one that they had just tumbled down from—was not a few feet above them. It wasn't even a few dozen feet. It was, by Sanjay's estimation, more than half a mile.

"It's preposterous!"

He squinted at the distant edge, then looked at Cider, and back at the edge again. Then he noticed the trees and crumpled to his knees, grasping his friend for support.

Sanjay was used to the jungle, having been born there. He was used to dense, thick woods. He was quite accustomed to old growth timber, so big around that half the guard would have to join hands to surround just one trunk. But what lay before him was an alien landscape, like something out of a fevered dream.

The trees were as wide as four of the houses in his village, and they towered to the sky. What appeared to be common varieties of small bushes were somehow as large as trees. What he knew to be grass was as big as the bushes once were.

"What's happening!"

He got to his feet, and found that his legs were shaking.

"We're in shock, Cider!" Sanjay clutched at his body, "we might even be dead!"

Cider knew that they weren't dead. He nuzzled his head into his master's leg gently and purred, to remind him that dead people don't feel tiger fur. Sanjay petted him as he looked around quietly.

Whether Cider or Sanjay saw it first is unclear. Cider's tail twitched involuntarily and his ears drew back as he snapped to attention. Instinctually, Sanjay jumped on his back and shouted, "Run!"

It was a gigantic Capybara!

The two spun around wildly, and Cider broke into a sprint down the ravine bottom in the direction of their village. The earth shook as the curious Capybara started on the pursuit.

"Faster! Faster boy!"

Sanjay dug in his heals in desperation, but Cider needed no encouragement. All his worst nightmares were coming true.

Tigers—even tiny ones—are quite fast. But even at his fastest, Cider was no match for the speed of the colossal Capybara. It was only by a miracle that the two somehow stumbled into a cave where the beast was unwilling to follow. Cider had spun around to attack, but the furry creature sniffed at the opening, then turned around and ran the other way.

"Yes!" Sanjay proclaimed triumphantly amid their shared panting.

Their relief was short-lived, being interrupted by a gentle, high-pitched sound of air escaping from somewhere in the cave.

"Sssssss..."

The two looked at one another, and Sanjay spoke.

"Did you hear that?"

The sound came again, louder and more distinct.

"Hiiisssssssssss..."

From a nearby nest in the side of a dead tree, a young Hoatzin bird watched with curiosity the hole where just moments ago a strange little creature had darted for shelter. It was the hole of the Mussurana, a snake that generally hunted other snakes. Today, a different sort of prey had stumbled into its lair, and the bird wondered how it would end.

He was not disappointed, for moments after their dramatic entrance, the minuscule tiger and its rider shot from the hole like a dart and disappeared into the underbrush, the lazy Mussuarana slithering after them with only the casual speed of inquisitiveness.

The path out of the ravine and back home was long and only vaguely familiar, fraught with strange and fresh perils. But with the sunset at their backs, Sanjay knew they were headed in the right direction. They didn't stop until they came to the high (impossibly high, to them) wood wall surrounding the village.

The gate was guarded, as usual, by a dual guard contingency. Sanjay thought he knew them both, but they were so tall that he couldn't really make out their faces. He thought it would be wise, rather than making such an entrance at the main gate as he would in his current condition, to use the rear gate instead.

As they made their way around, a new opportunity presented itself in the form of a gigantic hollow log. The log, it seemed, led under the wall that surrounded the village, a sort of drainage for heavy rains. Memories flooded back to him of playing in this very log when he was a child.

"Cider! We can go in through here! I haven't been able to fit through this log since I was a boy, but now it's as big as the largest tunnel I've ever seen!"

They cautiously entered the mouth of the log. A spider twice as big as Sanjay's head was suspended at the top of the opening, but made no move. Sanjay shuddered. If he could just get to his house, and into his bed, perhaps he would wake up from this nightmare, he told himself.

As they inched closer and closer to the opening on the other end, Sanjay noticed that the light was fading.

"Quick! I don't want to be stuck here in the dark!"

They quickened their pace, but the log seemed endlessly long.

"I think the end is closing! Yes, it's not getting darker, it's getting smaller!"

By now, Sanjay was panicking. He and Cider pushed through as hard as they could, but the tunnel seemed to be disappearing around them.

Finally—he could never say how—Sanjay and Cider found themselves on the village side of the fence, struggling to climb out of the small hollow log. Their large bodies protruded from the tiny opening in a most fantastically unbelievable way for a moment, before they finally burst out with a loud "POP!"

A village elder heard the noise, and came to investigate. An astonished Sanjay and Cider hardly understood what was going on as he started to address them.

"Here they are! What on earth do you mean, sneaking around back here by the fence! Why didn't you come in at the gate? We have three patrols out searching for you!"

Sanjay didn't know what to say, so he said the first thing that came to his mind.

"You're huge!"

The elder, who was admittedly a little plump, frowned.

"Don't you change the subject! Your llama's came back half crazed, with no one to guide them. They lost a good part of their Terra Preta running, and are still in a fright! I ask you again, what do you mean by sneaking in! And what's this?"

He reached down and grabbed Sanjay's uniform. It was stained with Pitahaya fruit juice.

"So! You've been in the groves, eating our fruit! You abandoned your task, and now you're trying to sneak in to avoid the shame!"

Without waiting for an answer, the elder grabbed Sanjay by the ear and pulled him through the center of the village to the captain of the guard. Cider followed at a respectable distance.

Though he tried his best to explain, no one would listen to Sanjay's story. Cider thought Sanjay got what he deserved, when the captain assigned a week's worth of extra supply duty, and deprived him of his fruit rations for a month. Whether Sanjay agreed I won't say, but he did learn this: if you're going to shirk your duty to pick fruit, you should avoid temporal disturbances, and try not to get juice on your uniform.

A Day Sometimes Pivots on Its Lunch Break

This story is written to represent exactly one day in one of the lives of Sanjay and Cider. It has a paragraph for each sequential letter of the english alphabet, and exactly one hundred words per paragraph. The constrained form reflects the main character, and is part of the story.

At exactly six o'clock each morning, Sanjay awoke to a narrow band, fixed frequency signal with an abrupt onset and intermittent sustained decibel levels. Most people thought of this simply as "an annoying alarm clock noise", but ever since Sanjay read Daniel P.W. Ellis' 2001 study on "Detecting Alarm Sounds", he couldn't help visualizing the spectrogram of the shrill, grating tone that meant it was time to get up and face the day. He wondered why the alarm clock manufacturers, knowing that their products would primarily be employed in tranquil bedrooms, designed based on principles meant for high noise environments.

Breakfast took precisely twelve minutes to prepare. Sanjay enjoyed rolled oats, which were slow to cook, but had an agreeable texture. The water took five minutes to boil, which is enough time to brush your teeth thoroughly and properly. The oats, tamped and flat in their measuring cup, were poured into the scalding liquid, stirred three times, and reduced to simmer for five minutes. While he waited, Sanjay would read. Then, the heat was turned off, and the pot was covered for two additional minutes. Time enough to arrange the bowl, spoon, and toppings: honey, molasses, dried cherries, and butter.

Commuting by carpool never completely suited him, but Sanjay had calculated the efficiency of the arrangement and determined that it would be irrational to discontinue. There were four people in his carpool, who split the cost of fuel, insurance, and vehicle maintenance. Two of these enjoyed chatting during the commute, while Sanjay and the remaining party enjoyed silent contemplation, reading, or other preparation for the work day. Only occasionally would the first two parties attempt to engage the latter in discussion, and only when they were certain that the topic would be of interest. They were all a good match.

Downtown was both pleasing and disturbing to Sanjay. The tidy grid was soothing on paper, but the clamor and commotion of the actual streets was unnerving. Sanjay was dropped off first, at the corner of 23rd and Madison. He would walk three blocks to his office—he could have shortened his route through simple optimizations, but he opted instead to avoid the stress of more crowded intersections. The final approach to his building entrance was an exception, teeming with people, but unavoidable. He would sometimes wait several minutes for a clearing, so he could approach the revolving doors without obstruction.

Entering the office building was stressful. The revolving doors provided a bottleneck, metering the flow of pedestrians from one side to the other. Sanjay imagined it like the narrow glass neck of an hourglass. In the morning it was turned one way, with the people flowing in, and in the afternoon it was turned upside-down, with the people flowing out. The two sides—inside and outside—were nothing more than the two reservoirs of the glass, places for the grains to reside as they waited to continue their endless inversion from home to work. Was he a grain of sand?

Fighting his way through the lobby to the elevators left only a brief moment for philosophizing. He found that by staying close behind one person and matching their speed, he could usually make it through the horde without brushing against too many people. He kept his head down, and swung his briefcase wide to carve out his place. If he somehow lost his front cover, he would stop and look at his watch or phone until he found a new target. It was important that he not be at the front of the line when he reached the elevator doors.

Getting on the elevator also presented a challenge. The person at the front had to press the button (which was most certainly riddled with germs), and manage the space necessary to allow the current occupants to debark before the next crew loaded in. It was a major responsibility, and Sanjay avoided it fastidiously. Any slot in the middle of the line was acceptable. Being toward the front meant he had a greater chance of finding one of the coveted three corners away from the button matrix (another catastrophe), where he could safely sequester himself for the duration of the ascent.

Happy to debark at his 28th floor office, Sanjay would breathe a sigh of relief as he wiggled his way off the elevator. The lobby was quiet and cool, and rarely hosted more than a handful of people. It was a place to pass through for most, but for Sanjay it was a destination of regeneration, a rare lull in the City That Never Sleeps. The receptionist sat behind a high counter, and by scooting to a far recess of the room, he could sit quietly and fiddle with his briefcase for several minutes without attracting any attention at all.

If he could stop the day right there, he would, but time waits for no man—especially not Sanjay. There were calls to make, clients to please, figures to crunch, and paperwork to be filled out. Always paperwork. Years ago, he had gotten obsessed with origami. Ever since, he couldn't help pondering on the massive zoo of folded animals he could create if he gave every report, every form, every letter over to that ancient art. The resultant paper wildlife park would  boggle the imagination. He would sometimes reflect briefly on the idea as he sat down at his desk.

Just as soon as he sat down, the work would begin. Sanjay often wondered at how quickly the emails, phone calls, and coworkers would flow into his mental and physical space, as if some giant work spigot were activated by the pressure of his butt on the seat. But this was it, the ladder-climbing, nose-grinding J-O-B. This was what he had studied for in college. This is what he had searched and interviewed for. And what wasn't to like? His tasks were clear enough, and he had the capacity to complete them. What more could he ask for?

Knowing all this didn't make it better. The job was hard. His days were hard. Even leaving home was hard. He looked forward to his mid-morning break. At precisely 10:30am he would mute his phone, turn off his screen, and pull a book out of his briefcase. Setting it down carefully in the middle of his desk, he would stand and stretch while he examined the cover and imagined the contents. Four minutes of neck, arm, and back stretches left him exactly eleven minutes of reading time. Others might spend the time in the break room, but not Sanjay.

Lunch wasn't for another hour and fifteen minutes. It would be tedious to describe his profession, so I'll describe a certain feeling Sanjay got every day just before lunch hour. In almost all cases, Sanjay was a solitary creature, ruled by a firm injunction that other humans were to be avoided. This he applied with religious exactness—except with Cider, a red-headed coworker from HR. She was kind, quiet, sincere—and yet personable and warm. He calculated his chances of running in to her on any given day at 48%; high enough for her to be a pleasant preoccupation.

Maybe it was because he liked to eat on the 32nd floor patio. It was a small patio, with a few plants, and several places to sit. Nothing fancy, but if it were any fancier it would attract attention and more visitors—and so it was perfect. They both seemed to like it, and would bump into one another. Maybe they both thought about the odds. It was certain that they both enjoyed meeting one another, whether by chance or design, or something in-between. This particular day was one of those chance days, when fate twisted their paths together.

Never did an hour pass as fast as it did with Cider! Everything about her was perfect, but more than anything else Sanjay appreciated how she made him feel as if the world really was good. When she was around, all of the anxiety seemed to fade into the background. They would chat about everything and nothing, and no matter how it went, it always went right. She would smile and laugh, and he would smile and laugh with her. She would cry and complain, and he would be indignant for her sake—but without feeling frustrated or disquieted himself.

On this particular day, a lunch hour just wasn't enough. Sanjay went back to his work on time, of course, but his head wasn't in the game. He couldn't focus. When the phone rang, he let it ring two or three times, rather than answering as soon as the first ring ended. When an email came in, he sat and stared at the subject line, instead of opening it up and getting right to work. He was, in a word, distrait. This troubled him, and he racked his brain for an explanation. Sanjay liked for everything to have an explanation.

Perhaps some aspect of the conversation was left unresolved? No, all of the topics had been suitably covered. Maybe there was something that they missed, some tangent that should have been explored? Impossible; he had analyzed each subject and outlined them in his head, carefully covering those areas that she overlooked. Could it be something he unconsciously missed? He replayed their conversation and found nothing lacking. Try as he might, there was no logical explanation. All the ignoring of phone calls and emails in the world couldn't make it make sense, but it was still true: one hour wasn't enough.

Questions still crowded his mind as work ended, and his focus on them reduced his focus on the crowds in the elevator, the grains of sand in the lobby, and even the crowds on the street as he walked to his carpool rendezvous spot. He didn't count how many strange people he brushed against. He didn't cross over to the other side of the road to avoid the bustle of humanity. As he rode home, he stared out the window absent-minded. All the while, a notion was fixing itself in his mind: Just one hour is just not enough.

Realization became resolve. There was no law stating that they could only see one another on lunch breaks! Sanjay fought back his anxiety, and found the courage to call her cell. She had given him the number once—in case he had any HR problems, she said—and so why not? Was this an HR problem? He wasn't sure, but she had given him her number. He hadn't really seen her or spoken with her outside their lunch meetings, so he didn't know what to expect. He was elated that she was as wonderful on the phone as in person.

Sanjay asked Cider on a date. Cider asked where and when. Sanjay, in his excitement, said they could meet that very evening at a restaurant of her choosing. Cider, to his surprise, accepted, and chose a restaurant that was quiet, and usually uncrowded. He could hardly believe it had worked! One hour didn't have to be enough, they could have more! More of that peace, that calm, that joy. More of that conversation that was worth calculating the percentage of having. More of something he didn't have any of when she wasn't around. Life could be more than it was.

The restaurant was too far to walk to, so Sanjay used a ride service. He didn't like ride services, because he never quite knew what to expect from the car or the driver, but he really didn't have any other choice. The vehicle that pulled up had dark tinted windows, and a sort of eerie green glow from aftermarket lights installed under the fenders. The driver was too friendly, and too talkative, and too fast, and smelled faintly of Patchouli. Sanjay drew in short breaths through his mouth and tried to look out the blackened window at the city lights.

Uncomfortable as he was, it was worth it. As they pulled up, he saw Cider waiting for him by the entrance, her cinnamon curls dancing in the neon light of the restaurant sign. She smiled lavishly as he paid the driver and got out of the car, then gave Sanjay a knowing nose-curl as she caught a whiff of the car's interior. He nodded and pinched his nose as the car drove off. Cider nodded toward the restaurant entrance, and without a word the pair made their way inside; the street was no place for civilized people to talk.

Variety was not Sanjay's strong point, so he was relieved when he saw some very familiar options on the menu. They ordered and ate and conversed. There was enough background noise to ease tension, but not enough to irritate. The light was cool and relaxed. Plants, and even an aquarium added to the general calm. Was it better than the 32nd floor patio? It was at least just as pleasant, and more so because there was no work to rush back to, no time limit, nothing else to think about. He couldn't recall when he had last felt this relaxed.

What made it even better was the apparent pleasure Cider took in their conversation. She was so genuine. When she laughed, it was jubilant. When she questioned, it was earnest. When she was shocked, it was sincere. How many people had he met in his life that couldn't manage this one thing: To be the person that they were, to face the world and present themselves, without hiding behind convention? Who didn't wear the mask of social niceties, sport the facade of learned behaviors which would make them acceptable? How much better this was, how much truer, how much simpler!

Xerox copies, that's what most people were. But not Cider. The two enjoyed what can only be described as a perfect evening together, both being themselves, both loved and accepted and appreciated. Though generally practical, Sanjay somehow knew this evening had been magical, enchanted. He got along so little with most people! But with her, everything was different. Somehow, he had to make this last forever. He didn't know how, exactly, but he knew he had to find a way. When they parted, neither wanted to leave. Their feelings on the subject were a perfect reflection, an image of unity.

Yesterday, Sanjay would have considered himself unlucky. Unlucky to exist in a world that he didn't understand, and that didn't understand him. Unlucky to struggle with imperfection. Somehow his perspective had now shifted. He knew what he wanted to pursue. Jobs and success never held much sway in his heart—nothing did, really. That was no longer the case. Cider held sway there now. He thought of her all the way home. He didn't stop as he got ready for bed. He still thought of her as he shut off the lamp, set the alarm, and crawled into his bed.

Zoos full of origami animals of every description crowded his mind as he drifted off to sleep. The papery beasts danced and fluttered and swirled around his office desk, which floated just above the ground of the 32nd floor patio. The surroundings changed in an instant, transforming in to the cool, dimly lit restaurant. He watched the stream of animals march into the aquarium, where they each turned to trembling origami fish. Suddenly, through the crystal water, he saw Cider's face smiling at him on the other side. He fell deep into her eyes, and in his sleep, he smiled.

Sunset on the Downs

"*Don't be too timid and squeamish about your actions. All life is an experiment. The more experiments you make the better.*"
– Ralph Waldo Emerson

His mom (who was named Ophelia Seven, after the constellation—but everyone just called her "Sev") activated the air filtration sub-cycle, manipulating the control pad with one hand while simultaneously removing and rotating the cartridge with the other. His dad (who was named Corvus, and who was something akin to the genus), less dexterous, struggled with the protective film on a household food pod. When she was done with her task, she whisked over and grabbed the pod, peeled the cellophane off with one swipe of fingernail, and inserted it into the processor. The man of the house smiled bashfully, and Sanjay, the child of the house, laughed.

"Dinner will be ready in a few minutes. You two find something useful to do while you wait."

Sev nodded toward her husband knowingly. For some time, the two had discussed ways they might be able to draw Sanjay out of his shell. Much of his life was spent working and in school, and what little free time he did have he spent reading. Little seemed to interest him, including friendships, hobbies, and even junior politics. They didn't really understand him, and so they stayed up late debating ways they might change him.

Corvus took the hint; this was the perfect time to put their plan into action. He didn't waste a moment.

"Sanjay, I have a job for you."

"Yes father?"

"The airlock seal is loose on the exhaust vent, just outside the main port. Mom is past her exposure levels for this sol, and you've seen how good I am at manual things—"

He bent down low, so he could look Sanjay in the eyes.

"Now, it's not a hard job. You just go through the de-con, put on your mask—always verify the fit with the pressure gauge—then make your way out the port. You'll be safe with your mask on. The exhaust vent is to the left when you get outside, it's the small tube that sticks out at about your knees' height."

He tapped the boy on his knees to make the point.

"Grasp it firmly and rotate it to the left. It will turn about 45 degrees, then it will click. Once it clicks, you just pull it out slowly. The gasket should come out with it, but if not you can reach in and grab it. Make sure the gasket is straight and flat, then put the whole thing back together. Does that make sense?"

Sanjay nodded. It didn't sound too hard. His dad smiled, then continued in a whisper.

"When you're done, take a minute and look around out there, okay?"

This suggestion came as a surprise to Sanjay. His dad expected that it would, but persisted.

"Don't worry about it, it'll be an adventure! Your mask will protect you, you've got a Level 3 with oxygen support. Now quick, go, before mom catches us!"

Though he wasn't quite sure why his father was acting this way, he obeyed. He liked to obey his parents.

The decontamination unit was adjacent to the common area, separating it from the vehicle docking port. In the decon, Sanjay entered the code on his locker and removed his Level 3 school mask. He wore it every day, to protect from the harsh atmosphere that was his planet's greatest dilemma. The familiar suction was evidence enough of its proper operation, but he checked the gauge just in case, as he had been asked.

He shuffled through the port and out into the wide world. Sanjay wasn't used to the wide world. Usually he would enter a conveyance in the vehicle port, the morning lift that would take him to school. He wouldn't even see the outside, except through the darkly tinted, almost black windows of the conveyance. While at school, they would be allowed play time in the Drome, a sort of large enclosed arena where they would play for a portion of the day. One wall and a portion of the ceiling was entirely glass, so that they could see outside— but the Drome faced the Complex, a series of enormously tall buildings that blocked all views.

And so, when he wandered into the outside world this particular evening, he was more than a little curious, just as his parents had planned. He got to work on the exhaust vent, so that he could explore as his father had commanded.

While he worked, his parents watched him intently via the security cam.

"Do you think he'll explore? What if he goes too far? Should we be doing this?"

"Relax, Sev, it'll be fine. We've already gone over it, the boy needs some adventure. He needs something to think about besides his books. His advisor told me in his last review that he even reads in the Drome, rather than playing sports. We need to shake things up for him, give him some confidence."

"But, the rules are strict, if a patrol spots him—"

"They won't. And if they did, so what? He's twelve, they'll just bring him back and we'll explain that he was out fixing the seal. Most boys would be out trying to explore by this age anyway. When I was twelve, Max and I could dodge patrols all the way to the fountain at Prime Square. We ran so fast it steamed up our masks! And we got caught loads of times, nothing ever came of it."

"Shh, look, there he goes!"

Sanjay had finished his small task. He checked the gauge on his mask one more time and turned to face the roadway. As it was dinner hour, no conveyances were on his small side route.

He had never "explored" before. His dad often talked about doing it as a kid, but the idea didn't really interest Sanjay. What was there to see? Since the Deterioration, the air outside was harsh and deleterious to life. Nature—a thing that he had read about in books but never seen—was a memory. What was the point of running around outside and looking at buildings and walkways that he could easily observe from a transport or skywalk?

As he wondered, he walked, and before long, he found that he had reached the edge of his dwelling cluster. His cluster had 20 units, each shaped exactly alike, painted exactly alike, and outfitted exactly alike. He stood at the intersection and glanced around. His conveyance would usually take him through to the east, toward the school. He had never been north or south from here.

Beeping sounded in the distance, and at first Sanjay thought nothing of it. It was just a routine patrol, nothing to worry about. Then he remembered that he was out without an overseer, an offense. He was out during the dining hour, another offense. He was more than one hundred meters from his dwelling pod without a conveyance, another offense. All those lessons on the laws and regulations came rushing back into his mind as the beeping came closer, but he was frozen in his tracks.

Finally, a story his father had once shared presented itself as a solution to his current predicament. In the story, his father and a friend named Max were out "exploring", when a patrol came whizzing by. The daring duo dashed down a side route and jumped behind a waste compactor, just in time to avoid the scan. Sanjay found himself acting the story out as if it were a scene from a second-rate play. To his surprise, it worked.

His heart raced as he crouched behind the large steel apparatus. He determined that he had had enough exploring for one day, and was about to head back to his dwelling pod, when he witnessed a most curious sight. Across the way, hiding behind a compactor on the other side of the route, was a young boy with reddish hair. That another boy might be out exploring wasn't the most curious part. The curious part was, this boy had no mask.

Sanjay watched him in horror. The Deterioration had stripped the atmosphere of oxygen, this boy must surely be dead or at least passed out in a few moments. The Deterioration had infused the air with toxins—he could name at least twelve by heart—there was no way this boy could live. Was he pale? No more than other red haired kids he had seen at school. Was he covered in blisters, or wheezing uncontrollably? He appeared to be in perfect health. How was this so?

He must have stared a little too long. The boy, perhaps sensing a pair of eyes glued to him, turned and met his gaze.

At first, Sanjay didn't know what it was about him that was so shocking. He was a normal boy, much like Sanjay in form and features. He was a few years older, but otherwise his perfect peer. Why was it so odd staring him in the face, so much so that he couldn't look away?

The face! Sanjay realized, all at once, that he had never seen the face of any of his peers at school, nor of any living adult apart from his parents. He knew they had faces, but they were always hidden behind a Level 3 mask. Education in a group setting required Level 3 masks at all times; they have the highest filtration, but they do obscure the features of the wearer more than any other type.

The boy looked at him, and smiled. Sanjay felt warmth and trust, and behind his mask he smiled back. Quite automatically, since he was used to his face being obscured, he waved. The boy waved back, then motioned for him to come over.

The patrol had passed, the coast was clear. He darted out and over to the boy. They both spoke at once, Sanjay in a mechanical, artificially amplified voice that came through a speaker mounted on the right side of his face shield.

"Where's your mask? Won't you—" Was Sanjay's comment, overlapped by, "You should take that thing off—"

The two laughed. Sanjay continued, genuinely concerned.

"Won't you suffocate? Does it hurt to breath?"

The boy laughed again.

"Why should it hurt to breath?"

"The Deterioration! The atmosphere has—"

The boy became rigid and started moving his arms mechanically, while he started a mock recitation.

"The atmosphere has been depleted of its natural oxygen, which has dropped to dangerous levels consistently since the

Great Deterioration. Mismanagement of massive pollutants infused the air with toxic amounts of Arsenic pentafluoride, Cyanogen chloride, Hydrogen sulfide, and blah blah blah."

The boy broke down laughing again. Sanjay didn't understand what was so funny, and it must have showed through the visor on his mask, because the boy became serious.

"Okay, look. If all of that were true, would I be able to do this?"

The boy sucked in deeply through pursed lips, then blew out hard. He repeated this several times.

"Nope. Good old-fashioned, unfiltered air. Just like our great-great-grandparents used to breathe."

"But," Sanjay dug around furiously in his mind for more questions to ask, but they all seemed to be answered by this boy's good-natured face. He trusted him. He wasn't entirely sure why, but he trusted him profoundly.

"I can't take you seriously in that mask thing. What's your name, anyway?"

The boy started walking down the street as he talked. Sanjay followed.

"It's Sanjay. What's yours?"

"People call me Cider. It's the red hair, you know. My name is actually Cian. It's Irish. I like Cider better."

Sanjay turned both names over in his mind. He liked Cider better too.

"So, when you gonna take that thing off? Do you really think it's doing anything for you out here?"

"I can't."

Cider laughed.

"What, is it glued to your face? Ha!"

The two walked a ways more. Cider paused as they reached the back of the dwelling pods.

"This is as far as I go down this route. I stay away from the home security cameras—see them down there, all neatly lined up? People don't use them much, since most folks are hardly ever out, but you never know. If they caught me out here without a mask—well, let's just say that it would mean an awful lot of running for me."

Sanjay was suddenly struck by the idea that he might never see Cider again, and the thought chilled his heart in an unexpected way.

"Wait, can I meet you again sometime?"

Cider shrugged.

"Sure. I walk around here all the time. Come out again and you'll find me on a side service route. Just shout my name!"

And with that, Cider darted across the main route and into another shadowy alleyway.

When he had made his way through the decontamination chamber and back into his pod, his dad was waiting for him with a wide grin.

"Well, how'd it go? Did you see anything interesting? How far did you get?"

Sanjay was still thinking of his friend, but didn't dare mention him.

"Um, it was okay. I made it to the end of the dwellings, then a patrol came and I had to hide behind a waste compactor."

"Nice! Did you have fun?"

"Yes, I think so. It was very revealing, I guess."

Later that night, Sanjay's parents stayed up late talking, after Sanjay went to sleep. They secretly hoped that Sanjay would become a little more adventurous, and maybe even sneak out on his own. It wasn't that they wanted him to get into any real mischief, only that they wanted him to be more curious—more, well, normal.

Sanjay stayed up late too, thinking. Who was this Cider boy, and how did he manage to go outside without a mask? Why wasn't he dead? Everything Sanjay knew about the outside screamed danger. He couldn't wrap his head around it.

At school, he used his free time to visit the library, and read up on the Deterioration. He read the most current literature and research he could find on the state of the atmosphere. He read the peer-reviewed studies, and the national messaging. Everything indicated that what he had seen simply wasn't possible.

He re-read the social code. De-masking outside a filtered dwelling unit was dangerous, and was considered a high-level offense. Offenders would be deemed a hazard to themselves, and rehabilitated in a secure medical facility.

So what of this Cider?

A few days later, Sanjay made some excuse about having an evening study session, and started for the port. His parents, guessing what he was up to, turned on the cameras and saw that there was no conveyance. They watched as he snuck out into the route.

"I knew it! I knew it would work! He's finally getting a little bit of spirit!"

At least his dad was happy.

It took several tries, sneaking out and making his way to the service routes between the dwelling pods, before he ran into Cider again. When he saw him, Cider smiled and called his name.

"Sanjay! I thought I'd seen the last of you! How are you?"

There was that radiant smile again, which Sanjay returned, unseen. The two waved as well, as was the custom, and then started walking. After some small talk, Sanjay burst out with the questions that were burning in his mind.

"I don't understand how you can breathe without a mask. How does it work—what makes you different? How do you do it? I've read all the most recent research, and it just doesn't make sense."

"Well, who wrote it?"

"The research? Various authors, scientists."

"Uh huh, but for what organizations?"

"Universities, laboratories, the usual people that would be studying—"

"Yeah, yeah, okay. But who pays for all those?"

"What? They're all Sovereign. Why?"

"That's right, they're all Sovereign. The government pays for those studies and that research. And where is it published?"

"In the Registers, of course. Where else?"

Cider kicked an errant piece of compacted household garbage that had fallen from a compactor.

"Where else? Now that's a good question. Where else would you look for research, beyond the Registers?"

Sanjay thought for a moment. At the school library, the only search engine available for research papers was the Register.

"What do you mean?"

"I mean what I say. Where else have you ever looked, in your entire life?"

"Everything is published in the Register, there is nowhere else."

"Bingo! In your world, there is no other source for information. One source, one truth, one tightly controlled reality."

As they spoke, the two had walked through several side routes, and darted across several main routes, heading north, and then curving west toward the edge of the city. Now, they were approaching the Barrier, a wall of enormous height that protected the city from the harsh Wastes.

"Look, I like you Sanjay. You're here, out in the world. Out of a thousand kids, you might find one roaming the streets during dinner hour. And out of the ones I've seen, you're the only one that didn't run off crying."

Sanjay felt flattered, but unresolved.

"Cider, you haven't answered my questions. I'm sitting here looking at you, looking at something impossible."

"So, now you're the scientist. You see before you something impossible. Perhaps I'm an anomaly, a freak of nature, an aberration. But I tell you, I'm not. Take off your mask, and you'll see."

"I can't."

Cider laughed, but in a melancholy way.

"That's right, it's glued on, I forgot. C'mon, I want to show you something."

They had reached the Barrier. It looked impossibly tall up close. Sanjay had only ever seen it from a distance. Cider searched around, banging on the wall in random places.

"Ah, here it is!"

Pushing hard against a panel, Cider opened a crack and jammed his fingers in, then popped the panel free with a CLANG.

"Here! In here, quick!"

The two slid into the opening, and Cider replaced the panel loosely.

"It's dark, and even darker through your tinted, light-and-life filtering mask. Just hold on to my shirt, it's not far."

After snaking through the dark passageway for a few minutes, they came to a loose panel on the other side, which Cider popped out easily. Sanjay held his breath. He had never seen the Wastes, but had heard that they were a putrid and terrible sight. He didn't know what to expect, but in spite of his colossal ignorance, he was unprepared for the sight that met his eyes.

The Wastes were, in fact, a wide valley flanked in the distance by dark mountains. The expanse was considerable, more unused space than Sanjay had seen in his life. It was strangely beautiful, though still ominous to his mind. The two scampered over a few boulders near the Barrier and found a place to sit. After some time, Cider spoke.

"There. These are what you call the Wastes. What do you think?"

Sanjay didn't know what to say.

"I don't know, it just looks like a lot of wide open space."

Cider turned on him.

"I forgot the mask! Of course you'd say that with the mask on—"

Without another word, Cider reached over and unceremoniously yanked the mask off Sanjay's head.

For a terrible instant, Sanjay thought he was going to die. He shut his mouth and eyes tight, and flailed wildly around searching in vain for the mask, which Cider had tossed on a nearby rock.

"Oh, relax. You're fine. Open your eyes, and tell me what you think now."

With no recourse, and only a limited amount of breath left, Sanjay opened his eyes in hopes of locating his mask.

Involuntarily, he drew in a sharp breath.

The world that lay before Sanjay's eyes was alien. Bright crimson rays of a setting sun, previously filtered by his tinted mask, streaked across the sky. Clouds, which had looked like dim patches of gray on a dull backdrop were actually silvery white, on a cosmic sea of deep blue. Stars, tiny luminous orbs, were beginning to peak out from the cosmos. Layer upon layer of color and texture burst forth, overwhelming the inexperienced young man.

And the valley! It wasn't a Waste—no, no one could ever think to call it a Waste. The rocks and sand of varied hues and textures filled the space between him and the mountains with wonder. But, where they only mountains? Squinting to stretch his vision further, Sanjay could make out something dark green at the base.

"Are those—trays?"

Cider laughed.

"Trees! It's pronounced trees, like the letter 'e', not 'a'. And yes, that is in fact what you're seeing. They spray chemicals on the ones that try to grow near the barrier, but they can't encroach on the Downs."

"The Downs?"

Cider told him of his home among the trees, a place that they called the Downs. He told him of freedom, and fresh air, and smiles. Sanjay knew, as he looked into the face of his friend, that what he was saying was true. They sat, and talked, and breathed in the air for an hour, as the sun disappeared into a deep purple dusk.

When it was time to go home, Sanjay longed for a different reality. With opened eyes and mind, it was difficult replacing his mask. It was torment weaving his way back through the drab, gray city, even with Cider's help. When they reached his dwelling cluster, the pain was multiplied as the recalled his beloved parents, and the contrast of his life with them and the open expanse beyond the Barrier.

"Cider?"

"Yes?"

"Will you come back, and show me more of the Wastes—I mean, the Downs?"

"When you're a few years older, and ready to transfer to your own pod, I'll come back. If you'd like, I'll take you to the woods—that's what they call all the trees together—and show you where I live."

Sanjay nodded, and smiled behind his mask as he waved goodbye.

When he got in the pod, his mother and father were waiting at the table. His mother rushed over and hugged him. His father gave him a knowing smile, and the three discussed work and school over their hot meal rations.

One Good Man
of Tribune, Kansas

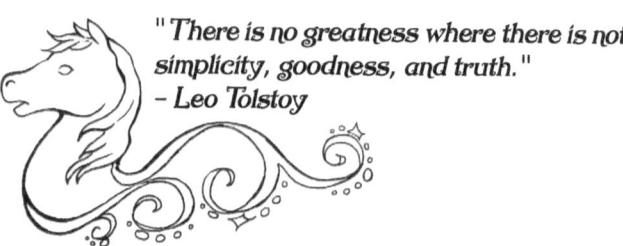

"There is no greatness where there is not simplicity, goodness, and truth."
– Leo Tolstoy

O n the dusty dirt road that ran by Jake's Texaco Station, a pickup truck sat alone. The windows were down, to keep the scorching heat from building up in the cab. No one rolled up their windows—let alone locked their doors—in Tribune, Kansas. Not on a day like this one.

On the seat of the truck sat a bag of well-worn tools. They were what we call Good Tools. So good, in fact, that I should probably tell you their story.

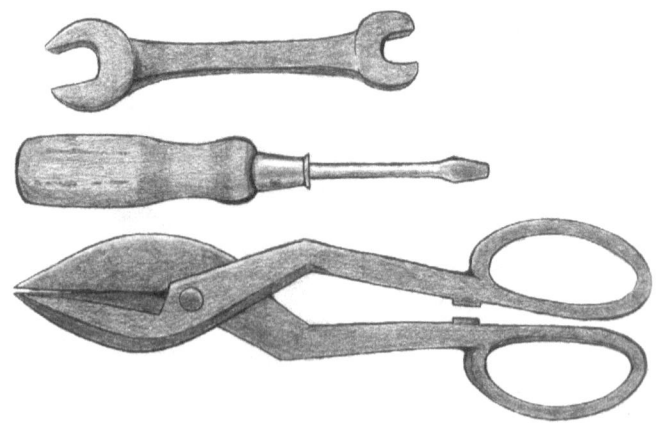

Tools need three things to be called "Good Tools." First, they need to come from a good factory; a place where the people in charge and the people who sweat, all collectively care about the product they're creating. Where they care, too, about the people who will make use of their wares. Chapman, Estwing, and Wilde—the factories where the tools in the bag sitting in the truck came from—they know what it means to make a good tool.

Second, after the last worker puts the last touches on a tool, it needs a good hardware store, a place where it can find its way into the right hands at a fair price. Sunset Hardware, on the corner of Greely and Broadway—the place where these tools were bought—was just such a store. When you walk in the door, they greet you with all the warmth that the name implies. When you walk out, you have what you need, and you know that if anything isn't right, the Sunset Lifetime Guarantee will make it right in a jiffy.

Third, to be a Good Tool, you need a steady hand a good heart to wield it. A craftsman is preferred, but if you don't have one of those, a workman will do. If those are in short supply, a handyman will fit the bill. Heck, even if all you've got is a pair of willing hands, as long as there's a good heart to back them up, they'll make as good a tool as ever you saw. In a pinch, you might well get a Good Tool with just this third bit, all by itself. The first two are needful, don't get me wrong, but truly Good Tools are only truly good in the right hands. The hands that used the tools we're talking about were so good, I should probably tell you their story too.

This particular pair of hands belonged to a man named Sanjay. He had spent much of his life in Tribune, though he was born somewhere else. People never asked him where he was from, and even if they had, it probably wouldn't have done much good. Sanjay didn't talk much, and when he did it was soft and to the point. He never got in a fight, and he never did anyone wrong. You could say that he was a gentleman, only his hands were a little too rough from all the hard work he had done in his lifetime. Most would have given him the title anyway.

Sanjay started out in Tribune the same way any handsome, young stranger should—by falling in love. He married the preacher's daughter, if you can believe it. After just a few years in the town, he was so well-loved that even the minister trusted him with his most precious child. The happy pair started straight away at building a life together, the best kind of life you can build in the Sunflower State. For reasons only the Man Upstairs knows, they were never able to have any children. But, they were as contented and cheerful as ever two souls could be.

As was often the case in Kansas in those days, the couple didn't have much money. So, when something broke around the house, Sanjay would set about repairing it on his own. When he needed a tool, he'd head over to Sunset Hardware. Good Tools, even at fair prices, cost a pretty penny. Still, it was cheaper than hiring someone, and he got to keep the tool for the next job, so Sanjay frequently found himself in the situation of spending money to save money. He found himself there over and over again, for years, until he ended up with a big bag of solid tools, hardened and skilled hands, and a mind full of knowledge.

One day, after Sanjay had retired, his wife passed away suddenly. He took it real hard, and started to keep to himself even more than before. People understood, but they missed him. They missed him at church, and at the socials, and at the diner. They missed him at the shop, and in the fields. But, Tribune is a town where people respect you, no matter how you choose to live, and so folks didn't bother him. Sanjay missed them too, but he was hurting too much to do anything about it for a long time.

Some years passed, and Sanjay found a way to pull himself out. He started to visit folks, just dropping by and saying hello. From time to time, he'd find someone who was working around their house or business, and Sanjay would take a few moments—or a few hours if necessary—to help out. He got to making a habit of stopping by old widow's homes, or even the homes of old farm hands he had known for ages. These people often had some little thing or other that needed fixing, and they were the least likely to be able to do it on their own. It made him happy again, to have something helpful to work at. And it made folks in town happy, to see him smiling once more.

He never asked for payment, and he never looked for any special thanks. If folks offered him a glass of lemonade on a hot day, he wouldn't say no, but he certainly wouldn't take a dime. "It's the Lord that set me on this earth, and gave me all that I have," he would argue when someone tried to press a dollar piece in his palm. "It ain't Christian to take money for doin' someone a service, mind, and you wouldn't want the preacher's son-in-law to be un-Christian, now would you?" He would use this argument, even though his preacher father-in-law had passed on many years ago.

Now, I can't say how long this went on, it was such a steady thing. All I know is, the story somehow came to this point— the hot day outside Jake's Texaco. Sanjay had stopped his truck by the road, to drop in at Jake's for a cool drink of water. As they were chatting, Jake mentioned that he had a transmission to drop, and that he could use a hand, so Sanjay rolled up his sleeves and the two set to work. A few hours later, when Sanjay got back into his truck, he looked across the bench seat and noticed that his tools were gone.

For a while he just stared at the empty seat. Then he went in and asked Jake if he recalled him bringing in his tool bag. He hadn't. Jake suggested maybe he left it somewhere. Sanjay was at widow Jane's place just before here, so they phoned her up. He hadn't left them there. "I know I had 'em," Sanjay said, scratching his head. Jake had a notion, and the two headed across the road to the diner.

"Come to mention it," Sally said when the situation was laid out, "I did see a car stop by there, in front of your truck, Sanjay. A fellow stepped out and smoked a cigarette for a spell. I do believe there was a fellow on the other side too who got out, but I couldn't see him."

"Well don't that beat all!" Jake exclaimed. "Ever since they put in that highway, we've been getting more and more of these folks blowin' through like they own the place!" He turned to Sanjay, who would never think of stealing so much as a slice of pie, to explain the bad news. "I'm afraid they've taken your tool bag, old friend. You won't see it again."

News of the malfeasance spread around town like wildfire, and in the time it took Sanjay to slowly and dolefully drive home, an emergency meeting had been called by Jake, with the Mayor's help of course. The two rounded up as many folks as they could muster—and as it was a case against one of the town's favored residents, just about everyone showed up. The crowd was hushed, the Mayor explained the situation, and the floor was opened for comments. Not thirty seconds passed before widow Jane stood up.

"Now, I'm not one to speak in meeting, Goodness knows. I'm all a flutter about it, but I just can't hold my peace, seeing as how Sanjay was just at my house this afternoon. He wouldn't want me to say a thing about it, and Lord forgive me for talking about someone who ain't here, but this must have been the third time this week he came by and fixed my old gas burner for me. I want to replace it, Goodness knows, but that will cost me and I don't have money to throw around. He wouldn't want me to say it, mind you, but Sanjay is there just about every two days, I reckon, asking if he can help out."

A rush of whispers went through the crowd, and another citizen stood. It was old man Harris.

"She ain't the only one. We ain't no gossipin' town, we all knows that, but a man's got to speak when he's got to speak. And Sanjay, so help me, has been by my place every Wen'day, to just help around, you know? We used to bring in hay together, and he knows I can't get much done with my back as it is."

People were popping up in the crowd like dandelions in a freshly mowed lawn. All around were stories about how Sanjay had served. Many saw a regular visit from the man, and by the way he treated them, they'd have thought they were the only ones. Still more had tales of how Sanjay had showed up right when they needed a hand more than anything. If there had been time, it's quite certain that not a single soul in the room would have held back a word in his favor.

"Something must be done!" Jake interrupted, walking up and standing next to the Mayor. "Sanjay ain't a rich man, and I know the cost of tools. He got those over a lifetime, and he's used those tools to help all of us. I don't know what he must be thinkin' right this minute, alone in his house without even his trusty tools, but I know what I'm thinkin'. I'm thinkin' that if we all got together, we could take care of this business straight away! Who'll follow me over to Sunset, and pass a dollar across the counter to buy Sanjay some new tools? I'm putting down at least two myself!"

A roar of cheers erupted from the crowd, and the mayor led the way over to Sunset Hardware. Cider, the store owner, was surprised to see the congregation in his shop all at once, but stayed comfortably seated behind the counter. Jake and a few others led small groups around to pick out the highest quality tools, of every variety they thought Sanjay might need to do any of the many things that he was skilled at. When they were through, they brought their hoard forward to the counter. Cider stood, and Jake started making a collection, as the Mayor explained the situation.

After the Mayor was through with his story, Cider stood looking at the crowd, thoughtful. Then he saw Sanjay walk in the door, and his mind was made up. "I've got a few words to say," he announced loudly. Everyone stopped to listen.

"You're all just about the best people a man could hope to know. And I don't mean any disrespect when I say that Sanjay has you all licked by a mile. I confess it too, he's got me licked by at least four. It may surprise you to learn, but Sanjay has even found a way to help me out. When my stocking boy was sick two years ago, Sanjay came in every morning for a month, asking what he could do around here. I had a lot on my mind—being as the stocking boy was my son—and I was grateful, believe you me, but I never did thank Sanjay properly."

"Now, some selfish fool has gone and made off with Sanjay's tools. You've all come here, willing to buy new tools, to show your thanks. I commend that, I really do, but I can't take your money, any more than Sanjay would."

Objections were raised, but Cider quieted them before they could get anywhere.

"Hear me out, friends! You're all forgettin' something important here, and that's the Sunset Lifetime Guarantee. Now, when I sold those tools, I guaranteed them for a lifetime. In your case, Sanjay," he said, motioning for Sanjay to come forward, "that means a Guarantee against theft as well. You come up here and look through what your friends have chosen, and if they've missed a single tool, I want you to go fetch it and bring it here—if they've got an extra or two, why you just leave 'em in that pile as a gift."

A lively applause broke forth, followed by three cheers for Sanjay, and another three for Cider. The townsfolk were so pleased that night, that they all took the money they were going to lay down for tools, and donated it to the pastor to fix up his chapel. The money paid for supplies, but the townsfolk, led by Sanjay himself, put in all the work for free.

Defaming Red Beard

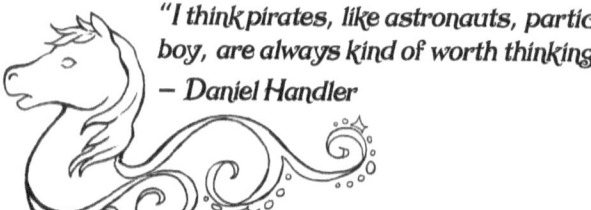

"I think pirates, like astronauts, particularly for a boy, are always kind of worth thinking about."
– Daniel Handler

It was a glorious, sun-shiny day, swathed in delicious layers of salty ocean air that came in waves, thick and humid. Atmospheric perfection mulled in the churning sky hovering just over the wharf, where the cool, crisp winds pressed down from the hills behind, and met with the sultry breeze that was the resolute breath of the sea.

There Sanjay stood, momentarily enraptured. He inhaled a chestful of the briny air, and held it for an instant, eyes closed. Almost on their own his palms turned outward, like sunflowers trying to soak up every last ray of the regenerative sun. Then, he burst into a sprint, his bare feet harmonizing across the weather-beaten planks of the storefront boardwalk like nimble fingers across the ivories of a pianoforte.

You see, Sanjay was what some would call a wharf rat. Or perhaps rabble, riffraff, street rat, vagabond, ragamuffin, or any other number of undeserved, dismissive, derogatory titles. He was none of these things. True, he was an orphan. True, he was a drifter. But, not a single malicious bone rattled around in his body. Still, he did what he had to do to get by, and for that he often found himself in trouble of one kind or another.

In this particular sea town, Sanjay had started off smoothly enough. He had stowed away on a ship departing from his previous home (he had had many), and debarked at this port to spend a few days. Or weeks. Or months. However long he could stay. He begged, worked, and generally made his rounds as best he could. But like every town before this one, he eventually got on someone's bad side. This time, it was Old Man Weathersby, merchant and shop owner.

And really, it wasn't Sanjay's fault. He certainly always felt that way, to be sure, but this time he just knew it. It came down to a penny slug—a small, round piece of metal that resembled a coin, but which held no value—that some cretin had dropped into his donation can. The despicable donation had gone unnoticed, and was passed unwittingly with a pile of other coins right into the greasy palm of Weathersby himself. Sanjay hadn't even gotten all the way out the door when the stickler's booming voice shouted after him, "THIEF!"

Quite out of habit, Sanjay took off. And what's a wharf rat —I mean person—to do, when the merchant of the town hurls such an accusation? Trying to explain it to the burly shop owner or the baleful constable would have been useless. And so he ran.

That was Tuesday. Since then, he had tried to lay low to see if the dust would settle or not. But, Old Man Weathersby was unrelenting. At every turn, either he or the town constable was hot on his trail. He needed a plan, and by Friday, he had one. Four ships were in harbor, and had been all week. Four ships were leaving Saturday morning, and one of them would carry Sanjay off to new vistas, new towns, and new possibilities. All he had to do now was to outrun the constable one last time. It was an easy task, owing to the constable's abiding love of amber ale, and before long, Sanjay had woven around piles of late cargo and down piers and docks, and smuggled himself aboard a fine vessel that flew a most trustworthy flag; the Union Jack.

Stowing away is not for the faint of heart. It's not an easy task to make it from one port to the next, unnoticed. But, Sanjay had done it many times before, and he knew all the tricks. He also knew that the laws at sea were callous and capricious, and so he never took chances. His ocean voyages were not without a certain adventurous romanticism, but by and large they were a business affair, scrupulous and deliberate.

Straight away, he settled himself in a nook in the cargo hold, between a rough bundle of rope netting, and a stack of over-filled burlap sacks that seemed to be stuffed with something light, almost like leaves. Just above him, through a chink in the deck, he could see the Union Jack blowing carelessly in the breeze. This filled him with a sense of security, and he drifted off to sleep, rocked by the delicate swells that would soon carry him off.

BOOM!

Sanjay was jolted back to consciousness by cannon fire, and nearby. He practically jumped out of his hiding place before his eyes opened. What he saw when they did open made him jump even higher. It was the Jolly Roger, brazenly flying where the Union Jack had been forty winks earlier. Before he could even contemplate the idea of a plan, the cargo hold burst open, and four rough sailors bustled noisily down the stairs.

"There it is, grab it!"

The three that were taking orders obeyed the one that was giving them, and rushed over to the bundle of rope netting that Sanjay was wedged next to. With all his might he pushed himself into the soft burlap sacks. The men were so busy with the heavy nets that he might have gone unnoticed, if his foot hadn't been caught in the rope. As they pulled the netting out, a stunned young stowaway was dragged along with it.

Bent on their task, the three sailors didn't even notice that they were lugging a boy along with their cargo. Sanjay slid on his back as they headed for the stairs, frantically trying to free his tangled foot. The one in charge stood, arms folded, watching his subordinates work. As they passed, he looked down and saw Sanjay sliding along the floor.

Sanjay smiled and waved sheepishly. The man's jaw dropped and eyes widened, and for a moment he said nothing. Just as they were about to start up the narrow steps, the man came to his senses.

"What're ya doin!" he shouted.

His subordinates stopped, and looked at one another blankly.

"We're, um, getting the rope nets, like you said."

"No, not that! There!"

He gestured toward Sanjay. The others turned, and jumped, startled. One let out a high-pitched yelp.

"What's that!?" they exclaimed in unison.

The man in charge stepped forward to grab Sanjay. As he was about to lay hands on him, Sanjay finally got free of the rope net. He rolled deftly away, then popped up to his feet.

"Get him!"

The three rushed to obey, but in the clamor two knocked heads and one tripped, so that the leader was forced to pursue him alone. Even with this advantage, Sanjay, who was unfamiliar with the hold, didn't last long before the large, hairy hands of his pursuer closed around his shoulders. The man lifted him off the ground without straining in the slightest.

"You're a slippery one, you are. Men! Stop fooling around and get that rope net up. I'll deal with this stowaway."

Sanjay gulped. In his few short years of surreptitious maritime migration, he had never once been caught. And to make matters worse, he had accidentally strayed onto a pirate ship flying a false flag! There were very few possible outcomes here, and they jumbled around his head as he was carried out of the hold and onto the main deck of the ship.

The sun was low on the horizon, preparing to set in a magnificent blaze of chromatic exquisiteness. It was a fitting end, Sanjay thought, to his colorful life. They stood still for some time after exiting the scuttle, before his captor spoke.

"Aye. I suppose that there's just one thing to do now."

There was hesitation in his voice. Sanjay seized at the opening.

"But is there? Just one thing?"

"What? Yes, just one thing for you mate, just one!"

They started walking amidship toward the port side railing. All about them, pirates were scampering hurriedly.

"You gonna toss me over?"

"Aye."

They approached the rail, and the man lifted Sanjay off the deck.

"You've got the authority to make that decision, do you then?"

The man paused.

"I'd say you'd be Quartermaster, that's what. You're no captain, judging by your garb. But, even at that, you'd be an ill-paid Quartermaster."

"I be a Boatswain, little stowaway, and that's handy enough in a time like this."

Sanjay noted another ship in the distance. The pirates were closing on it fast, approaching for a broadside attack.

"Ah, that's a disappointment. With your take-charge attitude, you ought to be promoted. Especially when you're making decisions that only the Captain or Quartermaster can technically make."

The man narrowed his eyes. Sanjay rushed to continue.

"Imagine the men saw you, tossing me overboard without even consulting your superiors. One of them might report it."

"Watch yer tongue boy, or I'll cut it out! Mutiny ain't a light charge."

"No, indeed, but neither is undermining authority. Maritime law doesn't think much of Boatswains that usurp their Captain's powers."

Sanjay felt his feet touch the deck once more. The man looked around nervously.

"Now, look here lad. We're fixin' for a skirmish right quick, and the Captain is busy enough. Now, you be a good lad and jump off here, and swim due north. We passed a small islet not far back."

The odds that they had actually passed anything but empty sea for many nautical miles were very slim, and Sanjay knew it. He continued to stall.

"I'm not much of a swimmer. Couldn't I help around here? Are you in need of a cabin boy? Or, could I just stay out of the way, at least until your skirmish is over?"

The man crossed his arms, and looked like he was about to have a few choice words, when the Captain suddenly burst out of his quarters.

"Shepley! Shepley, come to! On the double!"

Shepley's face dropped, and his eyes darted from Sanjay to the Captain, and back. Before he could do anything, the Captain spotted them both.

"Ahoy!" he bellowed, "What's this?"

Shepley stood at attention and saluted, as the Captain made his way over.

"Sir, Cap'n Cider sir! This be a young stowaway that I found in the hold. I was about to—um, that is to say, I was going to bring him to you!"

Captain Cider eyed the boy with curiosity. Sanjay was fixated, and for good reason; Captain Cider was the stuff of legends, the specter that parents used to get their kids to be quiet at night. His wild shock of bright red hair was eclipsed only by his red beard, long and braided. The story was that human finger bones were braided into those fiery whiskers, though Sanjay couldn't see any such thing now that the man was before him.

"Good man Shepley. Any other Boatswain would have scuppered the lad right quick. Too much head and not enough brain, you see. I'm glad you're more than that!"

Beaming, Shepley nodded.

"Now, as for this boy," Cider said, turning to Sanjay. "You can see, lad, that we're about to get mixed up in some serious business, which may or may not produce a scuffle of some magnitude."

Sanjay nodded.

"And, you'll understand then, that we can't have a mere infant who's barely weened running amok on deck, yes?"

This was an obvious insult. He was nearly old enough to take legitimate work, and not even close to an infant.

"And you can swim, like a good lad?"

"Sir," Sanjay began, "If I may be so bold: within a few nautical miles, you will overtake that vessel on the broadside. A few shots and you'll have it squarely contained."

"It's a fair estimate, given that you have very little experience with these things my boy. What is it you propose?"

"I'm looking for passage, and I'm willing to work for it. I could remain below deck until your scuffle is over..."

"Aye, but suppose you don't remain below deck. What then?"

"Sir?"

"Suppose, instead, that you decide to be the hero, and you scuttle the ship while you're down there, or set the powder kegs ablaze?"

"I wouldn't—"

"But, just suppose it. Now, as a responsible captain, I couldn't very well take that risk, now could I?"

Sanjay thought hard.

"You could tie me up!"

"Well, now that is an idea. But, are you saying that you'd rather be tied up during a ferocious battle, than take a swim? What if we lose the scuffle, and the ship goes down? Or burns up? No one will come for you."

Fast approaching, Sanjay could see the ship they were about to overtake. He knew exactly what he was looking at, and he knew that it stood very little chance.

"It's a merchant ship, they were in port with you all of last week. It doesn't have nearly the sail that you have, and most of the weight it'll be carrying is in cargo, not cannons. You've stuffed your hold with empty burlap sacks to look laden while at port—I know, I slept against some of them earlier—so, you'll be able to outmaneuver them from the start. Plus, crews coming out of port were scarce. I bet you had your men scaring people off on the sly. They won't be able to fight. No, they stand no chance, and so if I had to choose between ropes and swimming, I'd choose ropes."

Captain Cider looked at Sanjay for a few moments, then grabbed him around the shoulders, hoisted him high into the air, and set him firmly back on deck before responding.

"Ahoy, mateys!" he called out loudly. Several crew members stopped and looked their way.

"The lad has me bilged on me own anchor! I threaten to scupper him into the deep, and he talks circles around me like he was Admiral of the Black!"

The crew had a hearty laugh with the Captain before he turned back to Sanjay.

"Now, listen here lad. I won't put you in the hold during a battle, and I won't toss you overboard any more than I'd toss over my favorite gem. If you won't jump and swim, then you'll be a part of the crew, for better or for worse. You know what you're getting into then?"

"Yes sir!"

"There's a lad. We'll see where you can be useful later, but for now, I want you to mind yourself, stay out of trouble, and keep out of range, if you catch my meaning. These little boarding parties can sometimes get ugly, as I'm sure you can imagine. This is your chance to prove your mettle!"

Sanjay nodded and saluted as the Captain and Shepley snapped their attention back to the task at hand. He had wiggled his way out of one kind of trouble and into quite another kind. Just to be sure all was right within, he gave himself a good shake. Sure enough, not a single malicious bone rattled around in his body.

The attack and battle that ensued were talked about in parlors and pubs for generations to come. Details shifted with the tide, and some of the truth was a bit exaggerated, but the heroics were real. What really happened was this:

After receiving his hasty commission, Sanjay was handed off to Sheply, who grabbed him by the ear and dragged him back below deck. He was ordered to stay out of sight and out of trouble, then handed off to the Gunner as an assistant. A bucket of dingy water was thrust into his hands and he was told to, "go scrub something!"

As the others bustled around, he quietly emptied the bucket into the powder keg before hiding behind the nets. He was quickly forgotten.

While in hiding, it occurred to him that no good could come from pirate's nets, and so he took some time to loosen as many knots as he could.

Tense minutes passed, and Sanjay could feel the ship reeling in its attack maneuvers. The anxiety made him hungry, and he made his way to the stores, where he knew he could find a bite to eat while the crew were busy. Some cheese sufficed, but while he was there he found a bucket of lard, which he grabbed and brought topside.

The main deck was in the full throes of chaos as the pirates prepared to board. The ship had already pulled up next to its target, and some pirates were swinging across to catch nets and ropes while the rest prepared to board en masse. Sanjay found a free rope, stuck the bucket of lard under one arm, and deftly swung across.

On the merchant ship, Sanjay did what he did best: he hid. At the right moment, just before the pirates started their boarding offensive, he scurried out on deck and dumped the bucket of lard.

As the two ships met that day, the notorious Red Beard was plagued with problem after problem in his onslaught. First, the cannons wouldn't fire; someone had poured water in the powder! Next, when they threw the rope nets to crawl between the ships, the pirates kept falling through the nets up to their waists; someone had sabotaged the knots! Finally, after a few of the pirates made it across, they found that someone had greased the deck with lard; try as they might, they couldn't stand up to fight!

In the end, Red Beard had to cut free and sail off into the sunset, defeated. As he watched his failed spoils fade away, he saw on the deck of the merchant ship a young boy—Sanjay, his newest crew member—waiving goodbye. Red Beard laughed a hearty laugh, and was never heard from or seen again.

The Rubber Stamper

What a meaningless task at last! At last!
But why go on when you can go back?
Be done, be done, go into the sun,
Or into the moon, if you so choose.
Go into the future or into the past,
Will you be done, or finish your task?
- Malachi Lyman

Sanjay was about to die.

It happens to us all, great, small, good, and evil—everyone eventually meets their end. This particular Tuesday, it was Sanjay's time.

Of course, Sanjay didn't know this. For him, nothing in the world indicated that change was coming. In fact, nothing in the world had changed for him in the past one hundred years. Or was it fifty? Seventy-five at least? He had lost track somehow, somewhere along the line. If you had his job, you'd understand why.

Sanjay was what we call a Rubber Stamper. He sat on the assembly line, and as the product rolled by, he would stamp it. During his training, he had learned to lift the stamp, move it to the ink pad, depress it into the moist sponge of ink, then lift again, and depress the stamp onto the product. He had learned to synchronize his movements to the speed of the conveyor belt, which never changed.

That was one hundred years ago (or fifty, or seventy-five; it doesn't much matter). Sanjay had sat in that same spot, stamping product ever since. He neither ate nor slept nor moved. Well, except for his stamping arm; that part of him moved. Most importantly, he never thought. They didn't teach him about thinking in his training, so it never occurred to him. He was a Rubber Stamper, and that was it.

Well, that was almost it. He did listen. He liked to listen very, very much. You might say that it was his favorite thing in the world. There were many sounds to listen to in the factory. The sound of the machines pressing the product into various shapes and jamming it into packages. The sound of the product dropping from slider to belt. The sound of the conveyor conveying. If he listened very closely, he could hear detailed sounds, of metal springs and nylon belts. In the distance he heard motors and furnaces. Once in a while, he heard the back door creak open, and strange otherworldly sounds drift in; birds whistling, cars honking, and other assorted tones from memories long past.

Listening was his only pleasure. It was also the only thing that might save him on this particular Tuesday, when death crept up stealthily behind him.

You see, Sanjay had a highly trained ear. And so, when death stepped a little too hard on a floor board, Sanjay heard it creak. He didn't swing around to look (he didn't swing, he only stamped), but in his head he said, "That is a new sound, I haven't heard that sound since my boss stood behind me at training time." This made him think (something he usually never did, but this was death behind him, and so it's not unusual that unusual things were happening), "Perhaps I should say hello."

And that's just what he did.

It had been a hundred years (or fifty, or seventy-five) since he had said anything. The last thing he had said was "Yes", when his boss had asked him if he understood his training. Speaking was harder than he remembered. His beard had grown rather long (they do, in that many years), and his mouth was particularly dry. As his parched lips parted, he suddenly wished that what he was about to say would be "I'm thirsty, can you get me some water?", but what had already formed on his tongue was simply, "Hello."

Death responded, "Hello Sanjay."

Two things happen when you say hello to death (if you manage to hear him sneaking up on you). First, you're instantly transported to a place, nondescript, void, expansive, and dark. It's sort of like a big, empty room. You and death are standing there together in the dark, but you can see one another—you're both lit up quite well, though there are no lights to be seen. If you weren't so surprised you might look around thinking, "where is this light coming from?" Of course, the light is coming from you both, and so you wouldn't find any lamps shining down.

The second thing that happens to you when you say hello to death is, you instantly become a young person again if you're old, and an older person if you're quite young. That is to say, you become a middlish-age sort of person. Invariably, you say, "Where am I?"

(I say invariably, but the truth is that about one percent of people say something else. Some say things like, "Hey! What's going on!?" or "Who turned out the lights?!" However, this is rare. Sanjay simply said, "Where am I?")

Death responded, "You are nowhere."

Sanjay thought again, but he was very much out of practice. He looked around for something to stamp, but found nothing, and so, he began to speak. Death was a patient collocutor. Their conversation went something like this (though, I'm leaving out the bit where Sanjay asks for a drink of water and doesn't get one):

"What happened to the factory?"

"It's still there."

"Who will stamp the product?"

"For the next few minutes, you will."

"I will? How?"

"Your body is still there, stamping away. It's so well-trained, that it can do it without your spirit, at least for a little bit."

"Really?"

"I never lie."

"Who are you?"

"Well, my real name is Cider, but that always confuses people, so I've been using my title as my name. It's easier: I'm Death."

Sanjay jumped. He was altogether shocked, and not used to being young again, so he put a lot of energy into it. Though there is no official measurement, some say that he jumped a good four feet off the floor.

"Yowzers! You're Death?! Are you going to kill me?"

"It's not like that. You're just going to die."

"How do you know?

"It's my job."

"But I'm too young to die!"

"You're one hundred years old."

"I am? Has it really been that long?"

"Or fifty. Or seventy-five. It really doesn't matter. The point is, you're old, and you've been sitting in one place for entirely too long."

"But, I don't want to die!"

"Why not?"

Sanjay thought some more, and this time he really gave it his best effort. He scrunched up his face and balled up his fists. He tapped his foot and grunted.

"Because!"

Death laughed a gentle laugh. He had seen this kind of thing before, but he hadn't ever heard such a simple answer. The more he thought on it, the more he laughed, and soon he was roaring with a belly laugh that he hadn't experienced in millennia.

Eventually he stopped, wiped tears of joy from his face, and spoke once more.

"Sanjay, I like you. Most folks have gotten pretty opinionated after so many years of life. Most argue or fight or explain a thousand reasons why they shouldn't die. And here you are, a hundred years or so old, and only a 'because' to your credit, simply put, but with as much emotion as you can muster."

Death tapped his foot as he held his chin in thought.

"I tell you what I'll do. It's pretty clear that you didn't get a whole lot of living in while you were on Earth. Maybe you do deserve another shot. But, it won't be easy. I'm not going to send you back to stamp product for another hundred years. You'll have to do something with yourself, so that the next time I come around, you'll have a thundering debate as to why you should be spared a second time!"

Sanjay was getting tired of all this thinking. He groaned slowly as he replied.

"Ugh... I don't get it. What do you want me to do?"

"I'm going to send you back, but you're going to have to prove yourself. This is a huge opportunity you know! If you pass my test, I'm going to turn you young again, so that you can do something worthwhile with your second chance."

"What's the test?"

"Well, to start you'll simply have to get up, and walk out of the factory, never to return. I'll give you about five minutes to do it, otherwise it's curtains."

"You mean, I just have to get up—in five minutes—and leave? That, or I die?"

"That's all you have to do to get started on your new life!"

Death didn't wait for a reply. He reached over and tapped Sanjay on the forehead, and Sanjay returned to his body.

He inhaled sharply. The factory came into focus in front of him. His arm was moving mechanically, woodenly, from ink pad to product. He must stop it! With all his might, he tried to slow the motion down. For several excruciating moments it wouldn't break from its routine. The motion was too ingrained.

"I'm trying, Cider, I'm trying!" he thought.

Finally, the arm slowed. Then stopped in mid-air.

Next, he tried to let go of the stamp. His wrinkled, old hand didn't want to move. He wiggled it (he was too frail to shake it), but it wouldn't budge.

"Oh please! Please, help me!" he thought.

Finally, his index finger crackled and loosened, and he exerted all his will to pry it loose from the stamp handle. Dust fell to the floor as it moved, and the sound was one of brittle bones breaking, yet he continued. His middle finger followed in the same way, and then his ring finger, and finally his pinkie. The stamp was now wedged between his withered thumb and palm.

"C'mon hand, we haven't much time!"

The thumb eventually snapped open (he wasn't sure, but he thought he might have broken it), and he started to attempt to stand. If you've ever sat in one place for too long, you'll have a heart for his current situation. He had been sitting there for—well, you know how long.

Effort piled on effort, and second on second. Somehow, he was upright. By the magic of will power, he was turned toward the back door. He couldn't walk, per se, but he could shuffle, and shuffle he did, with all his might. The abrupt and abbreviated motion of his arms and legs appeared to Death—who was watching, unseen and unheard—like a sort of geriatric disco dance. Death laughed again, and was glad he had sent him back.

Just as four minutes and fifty-nine seconds were about to turn into five minutes, Sanjay stepped out of the door and into the sunlight.

He looked down at his hands. They were the hands of a young man. He heard a voice, coming from thin air.

"Just you watch yourself now! 'Cause I'll be watching you, and if it ever looks like you're going to sit down and do something foolish for another hundred years, or even just fifty or seventy-five, then I'll swoop right down and finish you off straight away. You got it?"

Sanjay nodded, smiled, and ran off into the warmth of the day.

World's Dumbest Superpower

"*I don't know why people are so keen to put the details of their private life in public; they forget that invisibility is a superpower.*"
– Banksy

Have you ever wished you had a superpower? It sounds kinda cool, doesn't it, to have a power that no one else has. Maybe you wish that you could fly, or lift heavy objects with one finger, or shoot lasers from your eyes. There's a list about a mile long of way-cool superpowers.

But, what if you had a superpower that was lame? Like, the ability to see dental cavities before they got real bad, or the power to sense when a tire is going to go flat. I mean, these might be useful, but they're not really all that glamorous. And, they might even be annoying. I mean, can you see it? You meet up with your buddy, and notice his teeth are in trouble, and say, "Hey man, you should probably see a dentist soon." Or, you're pushing a cart of groceries to your car and you detect that the lady you're passing will get a flat tire on the way home and say, "Excuse me ma'am, I think you should add some air to your tire there."

No one would call you a hero, they'd just look at you funny. Lame, just like I said.

Personally, I've always wished I had a cool superpower. And sometimes, I've even wished I had no superpower at all. That's because, from birth I've been cursed with a superpower that I just don't like that much: the ability to hear the Music of the Universe.

Okay, when I type it out, it sounds kinda cool, I confess. But once you learn what it means, you'll agree with me that it's more of a curse than a power. The Music of the Universe is a sort of soundtrack to life. You literally hear music in connection with events, places, people, things; anything around you.

When I was real little, I used to think everyone heard it. The music of going to the ice cream store! Hoorah! The music of Brussels sprouts, Boooo! People seemed to either understand my reaction, or react the same way, and so naturally I assumed they heard what I heard. I think I was about eight years old, sitting in a car on the way to go clothes shopping with my mom, when I said, "Ugh, I hate this song." The radio in our old car was missing (there was just a big, gaping hole there where a radio should have been), so naturally my mom was confused. We argued about it, and that set me on what my family called a, "ridiculous escapist fantasy," where I grilled everyone about the music. What a futile effort.

Since then, I've watched people to see if they can maybe hear the music, and I've even made some slight allusions to it. But, it has all been in vain. As far as I can tell, I'm the only one. Well, I take it back; some movie directors have it, I think. Sometimes, when I watch a really good movie, the soundtrack just lines up perfectly with the Music of the Universe. It's like they get it; they get me. I love watching movies like that. Most movies, when I hear that they just don't get it, I turn the volume off and the subtitles on. My family says I'm eccentric.

So, yeah, I have a superpower. It's just not a cool one.

Take love, for instance. Have you heard the music of love? It's amazing. I heard it once, with this redheaded girl named Cider, who was in my language arts class. She was giving a speech in front of the class, and the music started up. It was mesmerizing! I leaned forward, chin in both hands, and just soaked it in. I figured that this meant she was the one, so I approached her after class and made a complete fool of myself.

"That was good words—um, talk—I mean speech! A good speech! You did so good, it sounded like a choir—I mean you sounded like music—that is, I heard music—no, what I mean is..."

Anyway, you get it. My tongue fell out of my dopey mouth and hit the floor, then I tripped over it. Over and over. When I was done, I smiled feebly, and Cider—whose eyes had been getting wider and wider at my spectacle—turned and walked away without saying a word.

Oh, the music of crushing defeat and embarrassment! I could hardly eat a bite of my lunch that day, the music was so loud and depressing.

Of course, there are times when the Music is cool. There was this one time—it sounds crazy, but hear me out. There was this one time, when I was speeding down a hill on my bike, and this music starts up. It was this thrilling, compelling music, and it filled me with excitement and confidence. Then I caught sight of a pile of junk at the bottom of the hill, stacked on the sidewalk from some sort of house gutting project. Atop the pile was a wood board, perfectly poised to act as a ramp.

Nothing could stop me! The music told me that this was my moment of triumph! This was the jump of a lifetime, a moment just waiting to be seized.

You know when they say, "kids, don't try this at home!" Well, I'm telling you right now, unless you can really hear the Music of the Universe, do NOT try this at home.

I threw my bike into the highest gear, and peddled as hard as I could. At the bottom, I veered onto the sidewalk using an open driveway, then lined myself up with the rapidly approaching makeshift ramp.

For a brief moment, when the front tire hit the wood board, I thought, "Oh no, I'm insane!" But, I didn't have time to do anything with the thought, and before I knew it I was soaring through the air, screaming. Maybe I would have been worried, but the Music told me that this was going to be a moment of pure awesomeness.

And it was. After setting what surely would have been some sort of record, I landed the jump perfectly, hit my brakes and swiped my rear wheel in a wide, grinding arc, before finally coming to rest in a perfect I'm-a-rockstar-bicyclist pose. Did anyone SEE that?? As luck would have it, there was a group of girls from school sitting on a front porch nearby. They jumped to their feet, squealing and clapping. It was a little embarrassing, but I felt like a million bucks as I pedaled home that day.

Oh, and I guess I should mention that superpowers can sometimes be used to stop crime and stuff like that. Well, crime and maybe other lesser offenses. Once, this ominous music started up while I was standing in the lunch line. I glanced around and noticed that the class bully was about to push the kid in front of me; so, I reached forward and pulled the kid toward me, and the bully ended up pushing air, then falling on his face. I thought it was funny, but the bully didn't agree, and so he took it upon himself to educate me as to my place in the world, using his very instructive fists. A teacher came by pretty quick and broke it up, but we both had to spend the afternoon in detention. Have you ever heard the Music of detention? It's like an orchestra of clocks ticking. A fine reward for being a superhero!

There was this one time when I really did stop a crime. Like, a real one. I was at the bank with my mom, when this really dark music comes on. I think I was ten. By then, I already had the habit of looking around to see where the music was coming from, and my eyes came to rest on a shifty character who had walked in and was standing in the line. My mom was already at the counter, and the scary man was between me and her, so I did the only thing I could think of; I went and talked to the security guard. I told him that this man was scaring me, and pointed to the man standing between me and my mom. He reassured me, and said he'd walk with me to where my mom was.

As we passed the man, the guard did a double-take. He knew the guy! It turned out, this guy was wanted for bank robbery in two states; his photo had been posted in security and police offices all over the place. It was a confusing rush for my ten-year-old self, but what I remember is the man was pulling out a gun when the security guard swept me behind him and tackled the creep. He was lying on his face in handcuffs within seconds. I still remember the beat up revolver lying on the ground a few feet away, and the startled screams of the bank patrons.

I got my photo in the paper for that one. "Local Boy Helps Nab Interstate Crook!" one headline read. Superheroes in the movies get recognition all the time. It has only ever happened to me once. Which is totally fine; I don't think I want to deal with robbers and guns and guards any more than I have to. Or my mom; she was pretty upset that I had wandered off. "Sanjay!" she sobbed as she dusted me off and rubbed my hair, "You need to stay with me! Always! Right here by my side!"

Which brings me to another thing: have you ever thought, in all your wishing for superpowers, that maybe you don't want the responsibility that comes with those powers? Think about it. What are you signing up for if you get your flying or laser eyes or super strength? You think the Universe is just going to leave you alone with all that? Take it from me: it won't. You'll have your chances to do some good with those powers, whether you like it or not.

For my part, I guess I'll figure out what my powers are for, eventually. Maybe they'll help me win the girl of my dreams. Perhaps they'll help out when I have kids of my own. Who knows, I might even grow up to be a real hero some day, like that security guard at the bank. I guess what I'm trying to say is, maybe I won't always hate my superpower. For now, I'm just going to take life as it comes, and try to enjoy the music. It's not like I have much of a choice.

Man With the
Slicked-Back Mind

Sanjay adjusted the satellite radio settings on his brand new BMW 8 Series convertible, as he rolled through the posh neighborhoods of north Santa Monica. It was springtime on the California coast, so naturally the top was down. Warm air flowed past his sunglasses and through his jet-black, slicked-back hair. Warm ideas of making a big sale flowed through his slicked-back salesman's mind.

If you've never driven your convertible through the neighborhoods of north Santa Monica, allow me to paint the picture for you. The streets are wide, and paved with gold— alright, they're not paved with gold, but they are wide, and flanked by palm trees and lush verdure of every description. Set back from the road, behind generous sweeping lawns, sit monuments of preeminent architecture; mansions that could melt your heart and your bank account.

It was from these lovely abodes that Sanjay would select his target on this warm, sunny California spring day.

A lesser salesman might pick any old house. They're all rich and ready to spend, right? Perhaps the first one with any sign of someone being at home, or maybe the one with the most upscale landscaping? There are dozens of cues that any old salesman might pick up on and use in their selection of a target. But Sanjay wasn't just any old salesman, and he certainly wasn't a lesser salesman. He was the best of the best, a salesman apart.

Sanjay observed vigilantly as he patrolled the streets of north Santa Monica. His was a calculated approach, using specific parameters in a method he called S.A.L.E., which stood for:

S – Satisfactory. Financially sound; wealthy, without being ludicrously rich.

A – Accessible. Gate codes and security guards can't be part of the equation.

L – Lived-in. Not a summer home, and not a workaholic's crash-pad. The owner must be home.

E – Entrance. The entry needs to be situated in such a way that a surprise appearance is possible.

I won't tell you exactly how his highly-trained eye managed to spot the perfect S.A.L.E. (it's a trade secret), but I will tell you that when he saw it, his grin grew at least 2 centimeters wider than it had been in the past several months. This house was perfect. The grass was that length that bespoke of hired landscapers, without being so groomed as to suggest extravagance. There were no security measures between the road and the front door. The garage on the side of the house was open, with a car inside, meaning someone was certainly home. And the long driveway wound carefully around a landscape of thick shrubbery and trees, perfect for a subtle approach.

He parked his car by the road, grabbed his briefcase, and stole toward the front door, watching for signs of dogs and security cameras. Everything appeared to be going his way, and confidence filled his heart (salesmen have them too) as he walked across the front porch. His arm raised to knock as he took those final steps, when he heard a distinct click at his feet. His heart sank as he glanced downward; he was standing on a trap door.

There was no time to think. The door swung open under him, and he disappeared into a dark void.

Thankfully his descent was a gentle one, carefully controlled by a circular slide that eventually opened on a dimly lit underground room. He had almost no time to adjust to the lack of light before a hunched-over man in a dark cloak approached him from his left.

"I am Claude," he said quietly, as he snapped a pair of handcuffs over Sanjay's wrists.

"You are most welcome here, most welcome. We don't see many visitors you know. No, not many visitors."

Claude yanked Sanjay to his feet with surprising deftness.

"And where am I, then?" Sanjay asked.

Claude laughed a slow, hollow, maniacal laugh.

"Mwah ha ha ha ha! Why, you are in the Burrows of Bitterness."

He paused before continuing, "You didn't know that?"

He sounded genuinely surprised.

"No. I meant to knock at the house above."

Claude listened as he guided Sanjay across the black floor toward some instruments of torture.

"I see. I see. Well, here we are then. What's it to be?"

Claude scratched his chin as he thought out loud.

"The Iron Maiden?"

"Sir," Sanjay interrupted.

"No, no, it's too quick. Much too quick. The rack maybe?"

"Excuse me, sir."

"No—you're new here. How about the Pillory to start, eh? It's simple. Yes, and with just a drip of water overhead, falling directly on the end of your nose; for say three hours? Four?"

"Pardon me sir," Sanjay insisted. Claude snapped out of his evil devising.

"Oh, a thousand apologies. What is it then mister, Ummm —what was your name?"

"It's Sanjay."

"Nice to meet you Sanjay."

Claude reached over to shake his hand, when he noticed that Sanjay was clutching a black briefcase. He drew back in horror.

"What? What's that!"

"Well, that's what I've been trying to tell you—"

"But! But, you're—you're a—you're one of those—"

Claude struggled with the word. Sanjay, ever obliging, completed his thought for him.

"I'm a salesman."

With a shriek, Claude fumbled backward and tripped over a pile of spears, swords, and axes. Almost as quickly as he went down, he popped back up and started searching the folds of his cloak for his ring of keys.

"I'm so terribly sorry! Please, wait just there, let me find the —oh, here it is!"

Claude rushed over with the key and unlocked Sanjay's handcuffs.

"Please! I'm so sorry!"

Sanjay, who was used to this sort of thing, was gentle.

"Think nothing of it, sir, nothing at all. Now, if you would just point me to the exit, so I can knock at the house above, I'd be most thankful."

"Of course, of course! It's just over there, beyond the snake pit, the first corridor to the left and on up the stairway."

Sanjay thanked him and headed for the corridor.

"Oh," he said, looking back. "Where exactly does this lead, might I ask?"

"Yes, yes, anything! It comes out by the roadway. You'll have to lift the storm grate. I'm so terribly sorry!"

Claude's weeping amends faded into the shadows as Sanjay made his way up the mossy stairwell and out into the light. After dusting off his suit, he made his way once again to the front door of his S.A.L.E. house, this time carefully bypassing the trap doors.

KNOCK! KNOCK! KNOCK!

Sanjay rapped on the door with confidence. After a few moments he heard a shuffle, then the turning of a lock, and the door opened a few inches. A man stood on the other side, cautiously examining the thin sliver of Sanjay that he could see through the open crack.

"What do you want?"

Sanjay answered this inquiry in the way required by law.

"Good day sir. My name is Sanjay, and I'm a salesman. I represent the Allied Imperium Group, or AIG, and I'm here today to sell you some of our fine products. May I please come in and evaluate your product needs?"

Through the crack in the door, he could only see the left eye of the man he was addressing. Upon hearing the word "salesman", that one eye grew wider and wider until it looked like it might pop out of his head. After Sanjay's introduction, he waited several moments staring into that singular eyeball.

"Um, I said, may I please come in?" he repeated.

"Oh—yes, yes, of course. Do come in."

The man opened the door and motioned sheepishly for Sanjay to enter. The two stood silently in the entryway after the man closed the door.

"Perhaps we could sit?" Sanjay suggested.

"Sit?"

In his face, you could see that the man's mind was racing wildly. An idea flashed across his features.

"A drink! Would you like a drink?"

He started through the main room toward an open kitchen with a bar. Sanjay followed.

"Sure, that would be fine."

The man led him carefully over to the bar, then motioned for him to sit on a particular stool. Examining the seat, and the floor beneath it, Sanjay frowned. Under this stool was the outline of a trap door.

"No, I'll stand, thank you. I've already been to visit Claude, you know."

The man was aghast.

"I see. Um, well, how about that drink then!"

He rushed over to a cabinet and started pulling out tall glass containers filled with various colored liquids.

"Do you have soda in a can? I'm not supposed to drink on the job, you know."

The man did know, Sanjay guessed, and was trying to get him into trouble. This was a common tactic. Clearly disappointed, the man slowly put the bottles away and retrieved a soda from his refrigerator. Sanjay selected a stool that wouldn't disappear from under him, and sat. From his briefcase, he pulled out a variety of forms.

"Now, what is your name?"

"It's Cider."

"Thank you, Cider," Sanjay started filling in forms as he spoke.

"And how long have you lived here?"

Cider changed the subject.

"Do you play? I just purchased that piano last month, and I can't play a note. Could you?"

Sanjay, who loved to play the piano more than anything in the world, couldn't help but glance in the direction Cider was motioning. In a room just off the parlor there sat the most elegant grand piano he had ever seen.

"Oh, wow. Well, I guess we have time..."

His voice trailed off as he rose and headed for the room.

"Yes, plenty of time!"

Sanjay was about to sit on the piano bench when, out of habit, he checked the floor. There was an outline of a trap door visible in the carpet. He sighed.

"Really?"

Cider smiled and chuckled uncomfortably.

"The salesman who sold me this piano said I might learn, but I haven't gotten anywhere."

"Lessons! You need to buy lessons. I'll mark down that you need lessons. I'll have a teacher sent out starting next week."

Cider swallowed hard, then shut his mouth.

"Now," Sanjay continued, examining the floor, "I think if we do this, I can sit down and show you what you're missing."

Sanjay rotated the wide bench so that the legs were straddling the trap door. He tested it, then sat down.

"There we go. Now, listen closely, and you'll see."

He played a hauntingly beautiful piece, his own composition that spoke of Liszt and Chopin, with hints of Beethoven. When he finished, Cider was decidedly more relaxed.

"You see? You just need lessons. We offer a variety of private music classes in our Education Line. I'll sign you up for twenty lessons to start. You'll sign off on that, won't you?"

"Um, yes. I guess so."

"Good," Sanjay said as he rose.

"Wait, won't you play me another song?"

"Now, now. You know we have a time limit. We need to get all the paperwork done. And we still have some time to evaluate other needs. Let's have a look around the house, yes?"

Cider involuntarily clutched his forehead.

"I, um—I don't know,"

"You look a little pale. Are you feeling ill? I can order a nurse, we have a full line of healthcare services in our Wellness Line—"

"No! I'm fine! Please, let's look around!"

The two wandered around Cider's house together, Sanjay looking for anything that Cider might need to order, and

Cider tried to trick, trap, or distract Sanjay from his task. More than a few times, he tried to get him over another trap door, but to no avail. They finished their tour, Sanjay finished his paperwork, and the two parted.

Under the law, any salesperson who declares themselves to the owner of a property can evaluate the property owner's needs, and suggest a bevy of products offered by AIG (a powerful lobby group, and the largest corporation in the world). Those suggestions are sent to the Needs Assessment Group (NAG), a subsidiary of AIG working in cooperation with the federal government, who determines with impartiality (of course) which needs should be addressed, and which orders should be filled. That assessment is based on the income level of the property owner, and the condition of their home, belongings, and even the physical and emotional condition of members of the family. Thanks to the great skill and experience of AIG salespeople, almost all needs are approved (the NAG boasts a 98% acceptance rating). This wonderful system was enshrined in law through the "Keep America Buying" act, which sought to help more affluent members of society to do their part in the economic machine.

In Cider's case on this particular day, it was determined that in addition to piano lessons, he was in dire need of a larger piano bench that wouldn't fall into his "alternate basement entryway", window coverings that would afford him sufficient privacy (and prevent him from seeing salespeople arriving on his property), a bar stool stabilizer system (invented by one of AIG's own salespeople!), and an assortment of calming herbal tea blends to be taken daily, and twice on days a salesperson came calling.

Illusions of Glory

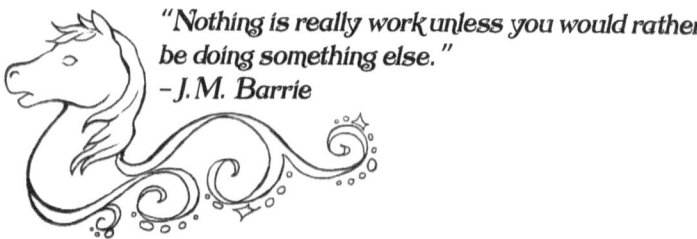

"Nothing is really work unless you would rather be doing something else."
– J. M. Barrie

Darkness and silence. A sudden flash; a bolt of lightning lights up a bleak city block. The music starts, the blackness gives way to a growing light as if the morning is dawning, an unseen sun casting its rays on a row of buildings. From the sky, letters begin to fall, landing hard on the city street and shaking the whole screen.

C... BOOM!

I... RUMBLE!

D... CRASH!

E... ROAR!

R... SMASH!

Lightning flashes once again across the screen, revealing the words beneath the name of the game's main character. The title screen is accomplished, and Sanjay smiles in anticipation.

ILLUSIONS OF GLORY

It was Sanjay's favorite game! The moment he got home from school, he dashed through the house, shouted out a short hello to his mom, and grabbed his portable game system from off the charger before landing on the couch and flipping the power switch on. In moments, he was past the title screen, loading his saved game, and plunging into the RPG world of Cider, adventurer extraordinaire.

"Sanjay?"

As he battled his way through a particularly rough part of the virtual city, his mom's voice came from another world to break him out of his fabricated reality.

"What?"

"Come here please."

Smash! Bang! Clear a path!

"*What*?"

"I told you. Come here please."

Hitting pause and groaning loudly, Sanjay got up and headed toward the kitchen.

"Ugh, what is it?" he said dramatically as he approached the open doorway.

"I need you to do your chores before you play."

"Mom! I just got home!"

"So did I, and I need to make dinner."

"Can't I just finish this level?"

"No. I'm making dinner, but I'd rather be reading a book. Would you like to make dinner so that I can read?"

Sanjay made a noise like a small whiff of air escaping a tire.

"Pshh. No. But why do I have to do it now?"

"Because it needs to be done, and we each need to do our part. Do your chores, and your homework, then have some dinner, and then you can play."

"I don't have any homework!"

"Good. Get your chores done, and then you can play, okay? I'm not asking for a lot here, Sanjay."

After a few more grunts and sighs, he shoved his portable game console in his pocket and went reluctantly about doing his chores.

Pick up his room. Check.

Clean the bathroom mirror and wipe the counter. Check.

Sweep the dinning room. Check.

Vacuum the living room. Check.

Take out the trash.

Sanjay made his way through the house, locating and emptying each of the small trash cans in the office, bedrooms, and bathrooms. He finally scooted around his mom and emptied the trash in the kitchen, before making his way to the alleyway behind his building.

"Stupid chores. Like school isn't enough of a chore? Man! I bet when I get back inside, the moment I sit down, she's going to find something else for me to do."

He slammed the metal lid down on the dumpster, startling an alley cat that had been hiding.

Suddenly, Sanjay had a thought.

"Hey! My chores are done, I can just sit out here and play. Then there's no chance of anything else interrupting me!"

He scanned the narrow alley, looking for the right spot. On the back wall of his building, to the right of his door, there was a small ledge. It was about seven or eight feet up in the air, about a yard to the right of where the dumpster sat. He'd seen neighborhood kids sitting up there before. If he climbed on top of the dumpster, got his foot in the gap where a brick was missing, and swung himself over, he could probably just about make it...

And he did "just about" make it—which is to say, not quite. He had one foot on the dumpster, and one foot in the gap where the brick was missing, and was just about to swing himself over, when the foot on the dumpster slipped, and he started to fall. Flailing wildly, he automatically reached for anything his fingers could find—and came in contact with the line that brought power into the first level of their building.

***

Darkness and silence. A sudden flash, a bolt of lightning, a pocket game console flying through the air. The music starts, the blackness gives way to a growing light as if the morning is dawning, an unseen sun casting its rays on a narrow back alley, tucked between two tall brick buildings. From the sky, letters begin to fall, landing hard on the alley road.

S... BOOM!

A... BANG!

N... GONG!

J... POW!

A... CRASH!

Y... SMASH!

Sanjay opened his eyes, and found himself lying splayed on the alley blacktop, staring up into space. What had happened? He remembered falling—and then nothing.

Then he remembered his portable game console.

"Oh no!"

He reached into his pocket, hoping he hadn't smashed it in the fall. It looked intact. He powered it on, just to be sure.

Instead of the usual title screen, the console went directly to a small image of a digital living room. His favorite game character of all time, Cider, was sitting on the couch.

"What the heck is this?! Is it broken?"

Cider's face turned toward him. On the screen he read the words, "Is what broken?"

Sanjay jumped.

"You—You can hear me?"

"Yes."

The words stayed on the screen, as Cider rose from the digital couch and started to wander around the room.

"I must have hit my head hard!" Sanjay thought.

He tried pressing the buttons, and moving the controls, but nothing seemed to affect what Cider was doing on the screen.

"This is nuts!" he thought.

Sanjay fumbled with the power switch, in an attempt to reset the game, but the switch didn't seem to work. There Cider remained, walking around the tiny screen aimlessly.

Then, Sanjay watched as Cider wandered over to a small image of a television, and pulled a tiny rectangle out from the stand it was on.

"Hey, that's the same place where I charge my portable game console!" Sanjay thought.

The screen zoomed in, and Sanjay could see that Cider was waving what looked like a portable game console. The words, "Now we will play a game." appeared on the screen.

"What!"

The screen went blank for a moment, then a new layout appeared. An icon representing Cider was in the corner, a status line with text was at the bottom, and in the middle Sanjay saw what looked like the alleyway.

"Ready?" appeared in the status line.

"Ready for what?" Sanjay said out loud.

On the screen, Sanjay saw a huge truck barreling down the alleyway. His stomach sank as he heard a rumbling behind him. He turned, and saw his fears materialized in the form of a two-ton metal beast rolling toward him!

He ran over to his door, but it was locked. Frantically, he looked at the screen.

"What do I do?!"

"Dodge the vehicles," in the status line.

He had to flatten himself against the wall and close his eyes as the truck blew past. On the screen he saw motorcycles, cars, vans, trucks—you name it, vehicles of every description coming one after the other down the alley that normally never saw more than a weekly garbage truck. Everything he saw on the screen materialized in real life.

Each time he dodged a vehicle, he saw a score float above the on-screen version of it. He fought his way toward the main road, dodging vehicles as he went, eager to get out of the alley.

When he finally reached the end of his building and hopped on the sidewalk, he breathed a sigh of relief.

Looking at the screen he saw,

"Level 1 - Clear" followed by a score.

"What! That wasn't a level, that was me trying not to get killed!

The icon of Cider changed to a laughing face.

"Welcome to my world!" in the status line.

Without another word, Sanjay dashed madly for his front door. But as he reached it, he heard a strange sound from the portable game console. He tried the handle, but the door was locked. Glancing at the screen, he saw the words "WRONG WAY!" flashing in red.

"Let me out of here! What do you mean wrong way?!"

He was frantic. Cider's face icon smiled gently.

"To get home, you must complete all three levels. Then you must visit Dale."

Of course, Dale! Dale Eggleston was Sanjay's uncle's friend. They had known one another since high school. He was a computer programmer. He'd made a small fortune with a game he had designed, retired early, and was often around his house. If anyone could help Sanjay figure out what was going on, it was Dale.

"Which way do I go? For the levels?" he asked, scanning the screen.

A green arrow appeared. It pointed to the right, up the street in the direction of Dale's house.

"Great! I can do the levels on the way!"

Sanjay ran, glancing down at the screen to see what was coming. First, it was potholes. Not the kind you normally see on the streets of Chicago, but massive, endlessly deep holes. Sanjay had a feeling that if he fell in one, he would never come back out.

"Jump!"

The words flashed on the screen as he ran, and he found that if he timed his jump with the commands on-screen, he made it over the potholes with room to spare. The first few were easy, but then they started getting bigger.

"No way!"

He came to a screeching halt before the last pothole.

"There's no way I can make that!"

He scanned the screen. A "Tip" icon and message appeared.

"Back up. Run ten steps starting with your right foot. Jump right at the ledge. You can make it, they don't design these to be impossible, there's always a way."

At that moment, Sanjay decided he was crazy, and turned to run back home. Then he saw it. In the distance, coming toward him, was a massive metal machine. It towered above the largest row houses and apartment buildings, and was covered in spinning blades, jagged saws, spikes, and all manner of terrifying contraptions.

"What is that THING!" he shouted.

"It is the Reaper. You must outrun it." was the reply, neatly typed in the status line.

Sanjay backed up, took a deep breath, sprinted exactly ten steps leading with his right foot, and jumped for his life.

And he made it.

Instantly, the street was calm. The Reaper had disappeared, and so had the potholes. The screen read, "Level 2 – Clear" followed by an even higher score.

"I'm almost there! His house is just around the corner..."

"Yes," came the typed reply, "Now, on to Level 3."

Another green arrow flashed, pointing toward Dale's house. The sound of a car horn startled him. Sanjay looked up, and noticed that the street had become completely jammed with cars. Glancing around, he saw that the sidewalk was packed with pedestrians, so many that you couldn't see a way through.

"What is this level?" he said out loud.

A title appeared on the screen.

"Level 3 – Rooftop Dash"

Sanjay's stomach lurched.

"What do you mean? What in the world does that mean?!"

A door on one of the apartment buildings swung open, the green arrow urging him onward.

Inside, Sanjay found a stairwell, which led him to the roof of the building.

"No way!" he said, as he approached the edge of the roof.

"This arrow points off the edge? What is this?"

The word, "Jump" appeared in the status line.

"Jump? To the next roof? Are you insane?"

"They don't design these to be impossible, there's always a way." appeared in response.

Sanjay's head swam as he peered over the edge at the tiny cars and people below. The next roof was perhaps close enough to reach. But who would be crazy enough to try it?

And then he heard it. He didn't have to turn to know that the clanking, grinding, whirring sound was the Reaper, coming to help move him along—but he did turn. It was about a block away.

"Right. Okay, let's do this. What are the tips?"

"Sorry, you used your cheat on the last level," came the reply.

"What! I didn't even know that was a thing!"

"Sorry."

"This is crazy, I'm not doing it!"

In a rage, he drew his arm back, ready to throw the portable game console off the rooftop, when it started to beep wildly. He paused, and glanced at the screen.

"INCOMING!"

The word flashed in red. Sanjay had played enough video games to know what it meant. He looked to the sky, and saw great fireballs hurtling toward him!

He ran. He jumped. Somehow, impossibly, he landed on the next rooftop, And then the next. The Reaper was closing in, and fire was raining down, and it was all he could do to keep his sanity. But, he made it. Finally, he landed and rolled on what he thought was the roof of Dale's house.

The sky cleared. The sound of the Reaper disappeared. Breathing heavily, he lifted the game console and read the words: "Level 3 – Clear!"

For a brief instant he was relieved. But then the screen went blank, and he saw:

BOSS FIGHT: DALE vs SANJAY

"Noooooo!"

His scream was drowned out by a loud rumbling sound, as the house he was standing on began to shake, and a giant hole crumbled in the center of the roof. Out of it floated Dale—or rather, some monstrous beast that clearly looked like Dale, except ten times larger and with giant muscly arms holding menacing weapons, eyes glowing red, and a mouth that breathed fire.

"I won't do it! I said no! That's, this is the last straw!"

Sanjay ran for the edge. He thought about jumping, but it was three stories. The screen flashed "WRONG WAY!"

"I don't care!"

Without another word, he jammed the portable game console in his pocket, and started to climb over the ledge. Bleeps and bloops were emanating wildly out of his pants, evidence of the device's madness. Though he tried, his attempt to escape was doomed to failure; it just wasn't part of the game. Sanjay slipped, and fell. Flailing wildly, he automatically reached for anything his fingers could find— and came in contact with the line that brought power into the third level of Dale's building.

***

Sanjay's eyes opened slowly. He had respawned in his living room! He had no idea how it happened, but he had played enough video games to know that it had in fact happened. He pulled the portable game console out of his pocket and looked at the black screen. Did he dare power it on?

His pulse raced as curiosity overcame trepidation. He powered up the unit, and palpably felt the milliseconds crawl by. He breathed a sigh of relief as the letters began to fall; it was the normal title screen of CIDER, ILLUSIONS OF GLORY.

He powered down the game and set the console carefully in the charging cradle. He wasn't in the mood for video games.

"Sanjay?"

The sound of plates being set and the smell of spaghetti made him realize just how thankful he was for a simple, understandable, and unmistakable reality. He rushed to the kitchen, and wrapped his arms around his mom in a tight hug as she set the table.

"Well! You're certainly all cozy. What gives? Did you go around the building or something? I didn't see you come back in the back door, but you were only gone half a minute, how could you get around the block so fast?"

A lump was in his throat. He couldn't begin to explain, but he felt he had to say something.

"I'm sorry for complaining about the chores, mom. Is there anything else I can help with?"

He's Your Dog Now

"Dwell on the beauty of life. Watch the stars, and see yourself running with them."
- Marcus Aurelius

Sunlight glinted in bright white bursts from the polished chrome of the pushrims. The camber of the wheels, seat pad height, front rigging and casters—everything about the wheelchair spoke of perfection. His dad beamed as Sanjay inspected it lazily from the front porch swing.

"I talked to professionals, this thing is top of the line! It's an athletic chair, not one of those kinds to get pushed around in. They do races, track meets, they even play basketball in these things!"

He glanced from Sanjay to the chair, and back again. The rope of the swing creaked lazily in the breeze, but Sanjay didn't stir.

"The wheels are carbon fiber! And these pushrims are fitted to your hand size, totally not stock—plus, I got these grips that you can add—"

"I like my walker," Sanjay interrupted.

"Your walker? Yeah, sure, okay—but you can't run in that thing!"

"I can't run in that thing either. And if I don't work on my legs, they'll never get strong again."

His dad closed his eyes and sighed, and for a brief moment, Sanjay felt sorry for someone other than himself. It was clear his dad had put a lot of thought into this gift, and it was clear that he had spared no expense. They didn't have a lot of money, and this must have set him back at least a whole paycheck.

"Dad, I'm sorry. I like it, I really do. It's just not going to change anything. I love to run, and you're talking about something completely different."

"Yeah, but—if you'd just look at what you could do—just think about all the things that are still open to you!"

They would have beaten the dead horse yet again, if Sanjay's mom hadn't stuck her head out of the screen door and coughed, then waved for his dad to come in. She spoke in whispers, but Sanjay knew what she was saying.

"It's not his fault."

"He just needs time."

"Don't push the boy."

"He needs to learn to be a new person."

"You can't replace what he lost."

"Let him do this his way."

"Be patient."

Ever since the accident, they had had countless conversations about how he might never run again. Star athlete on his high school varsity track team, state champion in multiple events, full-ride scholarship to one of the best schools in the Midwest—and he might never run again.

The words crashed in his mind like a thousand steel pipes tumbling onto concrete. He heard them when he woke up, and when he went to bed. He even heard them in his dreams.

"You might never run again."

Doctors too, in Sanjay's waking nightmares, would tell him the same thing. Some were blunt, others tried to soften the blow, but the message was always the same.

"You might never run again."

His head and heart ached from dwelling on it, and a bitter lump was slowly forming in his throat when his mom finally came out. She paused in the doorway, smiling faintly at Sanjay, then walked over and knelt in front of him, taking his hand. His heart always melted when she did that.

"Sweetheart, I know it's hard."

She always knew. Moms always do.

"Your dad's just trying, alright? He wants to help, and he doesn't know how."

The lump in his throat was getting harder, but he didn't want to cry.

"I know," Sanjay replied. "Tell him I know, will you?"

His mom smiled and nodded.

When his dad came down to the dinner table that night, Sanjay was sitting in his new chair. He flipped a brief wheelie when he saw his dad pause at the bottom of the stairs. A smiled beamed on his father's face.

"Very nice, son! Very nice!"

***

The chrome on his pushrims was smudged and scratched from months of hard use. He had quite gotten used to the chair, and had even learned to love it. A ramp was built to help him get down from the porch on his own, and Sanjay was feeling more self-reliant than he had felt since the accident.

High school graduation had come and gone. His friends cheered so loud when he rolled across the platform to receive his diploma, that for an instant the steel crashing was drowned out and his heart was light. The university had sent a special representative out to talk with him about his scholarship, and how they had converted it to a scholarship program for a different—a special—athletics program. They were nice at flowering up the words, but it was hard to hear. Hard to hear over the crashing steel.

They say that time heals all wounds, but for Sanjay, time wasn't helping yet. He was "moving on," as they say, but his heart was still a lead lump in his chest, and the dreams still woke him up in a cold sweat. The words. He couldn't help thinking that he was missing something, something that no one else could understand.

It was a fine summer day that Old Man Cider chose to pay a visit. Sanjay had known him as their recluse neighbor, a "fine old gentleman, best that you ever could know," as people would call him, but not someone to pay visits. He hadn't even heard anyone mention him for years, it seemed. And so, when Sanjay saw him approaching, he forgot his manners and yelled out from the porch swing,

"Ain't nobody home here, Mr. Cider!"

Cider paused and looked around for a moment, confused perhaps that a voice was declaring that no one was there.

"I mean, mom and dad aren't at home, sir! They've gone to the city, won't be back for a few days."

Without a reply, Cider dropped his head and started toward the house once again. His was more than just the languid slowness of old age. With each step he labored, dragging one stiff, obstinate leg forward which he let buckle under his weight for only a moment. The other leg, more cooperative, shuffled forward to take the load off, and the whole process started over. An old dog trailed behind him in his colossal shadow—for he was, or had been, a colossal man.

"Heard about the accident," he said, breathing heavily between words, when he finally reached the porch steps. "Thought I might help."

Sanjay had no idea what he was talking about, but couldn't even think to ask. Who was this man, who showed up more than a year late to give his condolences?

Cider gave a light whistle, and the dog that was behind him came slowly around. Sanjay recognized that it was an old greyhound.

"He's yours," Cider declared flatly.

For a while the only sound was Cider's slow, heavy breathing, and the wind in the top of the old tree. Then Sanjay grasped on to some sense, but not his manners, and blurted out a question.

"What do you mean?"

"Well, I mean he's your dog now. He's a good dog, he's been with me ever since—forever, I suppose."

"Um—I, well, I mean—thank you. But, you don't need to do that. I'm heading off to college soon, actually."

"Yeah," Cider sighed, "I know. Maybe it'll be hard to take him, maybe it won't. S'up to you. Don't matter much anyhow, he's your dog now."

With that, Cider turned and started on his arduous trek down the front walk to the road. The dog stayed put.

"But, I can't just take your dog Mr. Cider, it..." His words trailed off. Sanjay couldn't think of a reason to say no.

"I don't even know his name!"

Cider paused and turned around. He looked dazed.

"His name? His name... I don't suppose I ever thought of giving him one."

He laughed. It was a chuckle at first, then it seemed to resonate louder as his belly jiggled.

"No, I never thought to, son. You do that, if you want to. Give him whatever name you think suits him best, I guess."

Dumbfounded, Sanjay just stared as the old man made his way to the road and turned to head home. It must have been at least ten minutes before Sanjay finally turned his attention back to the dog.

His heart skipped a beat.

The dog wasn't an old greyhound at all, but a young one, not more than a couple years old. Had his eyes been playing tricks on him? This dog was a fine specimen. His clean, glossy coat was a dark amber-red, not even thick enough to conceal the taut, lean muscles beneath it. Sanjay eyed him curiously.

"Well, I guess we'll have to start by giving you a name."

He puzzled for a few moments, then it hit him.

"Hey, I know! You look more like a 'Cider' than Old Man Cider does, by a mile! Look at that coat! In memory of him, I'll call you Cider!"

Sanjay clicked his tongue to call Cider over. Cider rose very deliberately from sitting to standing on all fours. He moved slowly, faltering, struggling to climb the porch steps. Finally, he arrived at Sanjay's side.

"Ah, I see. That must be why I thought you were an old dog. You certainly move around like one."

Cider wagged his tail.

"That's alright, I move around like an old dog too, boy. Come on, I'll grab my walker and show you around the place. My parents are out of town for a few days, it'll be nice to have company."

Cider was patient with the tour, even though it was an obvious exertion. Sanjay didn't notice, really, having become so used to exertion himself.

"My room used to be up the stairs, but we moved it down here."

"This is the kitchen, I doubt mom will ever let you in here again, so have a good look."

"Dinning room. If you're quiet, I bet you could probably get away with sitting under the table while we eat. Then I could pass you the things I don't like. You're not picky, are you?"

"Here's the living room. Stay off the furniture, or mom will have a fit."

"My room. Our room. You can climb on whatever you want in here. The bed is nice and low, makes it easier for me. Probably make it easier for you too. Try it."

After the tour, the two ended once again on the front porch. Sanjay transferred from his walker to his chair. Cider sat patiently and watched.

"You sure are an obedient dog. You do whatever I say, and sometimes you do what you should without me saying a thing. He must have trained you well. C'mon, I'll show you the yard."

Sanjay made his way down the ramp, and on to the concrete of the front walk. Cider followed, slowly. When he caught up, the two rolled and walked haltingly to the road.

In the distance, a rumble and a whistle announced a rapidly approaching train.

"That's the train. You probably heard it from Old Man Cider's place, but it's a lot closer right here. The tracks pass by just over there, at the edge of the field."

Cider sat, his tail wagging rapidly.

"You want to go watch it pass by?"

His tail swept the concrete at an alarming rate.

"Okay, let's go, it's not far."

The two made their way down the bumpy sidewalk, and stopped by the railroad crossing sign. The train was a fast one, a commuter train bustling folks from one place to the next just as quickly as it could.

Cider had automatically sat himself down once again, his tail flickering wildly.

"Now, you just stay right there, boy. These trains go quick, you gotta be careful."

The clatter of steel on steel rushed closer, and the dog's tail threatened to fly right off.

"Calm down, it'll be here and past in no time. It'll be fun to watch."

Cider was panting now, his body twitching. And then, the train burst past them, a mass of steel and fury and passengers in a hurry.

Though it was moving quickly, Sanjay couldn't help noticing that on the side of the engine, right before the large identifying numbers, was a logo. He hadn't ever paid any attention to it before, but today it stood out to him and he recalled instantly that the train line was named, "White Hare Expressway." The logo was an image of a hare sprinting.

Cider bolted!

Never had Sanjay seen a dog go from zero to mad dash in such a hurry. Cider was in hot pursuit of his instincts, his dreams, and his desires.

"Wait boy! Stop! Ciiiideeeer!"

Thoughts and questions and frustrations flew through Sanjay's head instantaneously.

"What is he doing?!"

"How is he doing that?!"

"Old Man Cider is going to kill me!"

"My dad is going to kill me!"

"Come back Cider!"

And almost as quickly as his thoughts, Sanjay started pushing across the road and into the field, in mad pursuit of the mad dog. His arms flew, fingers making contact with pushrims in a wild frenzy that must have looked like something out of a cartoon.

But it was no use. Cider was too fast.

Then, Sanjay hit a rock, and flew out of his chair.

"Stupid dog! You're going to get yourself killed!"

He got up on his hands and knees, and started crawling in the direction of the runaway greyhound. Tears were streaming down his face.

"Ciiiiideeeeer!" he called out, his voice cracking.

His hand twisted in a hole, and he fell on his face. He rose carefully to his feet, balancing, cursing. Looking into the distance, he saw the dog, still chasing the White Hare. Sanjay cupped his hands to his mouth and called out once again.

Then he stumbled forward, and caught his balance again, his eyes fixed on the dog growing smaller in the distance. He ventured a step—it felt like a catastrophe, but he did not fall. Another, and another. He was walking, calling, crying.

His pace quickened, his feet tapping out a familiar rhythm on the dry path of ground at the edge of the corn field.He was walking.

He was jogging.

He was running.

As soon as he felt it—that pace, that groove that he knew in his soul, from the tips of his toes to the top of his head— nothing could hold him back. He burst into a sprint, confident, alive. He ran harder and faster than he had ever known.

You will run again!

The words. The clattering of falling steel transformed into the rushing of wind and the sound of the cheering crowd.

You will run again!

And somehow, he was catching up with Cider! He couldn't explain it, but he knew it. He pushed, and his body went faster, and faster, and faster. Now, Cider wasn't a speck in the distance. Now, Cider wasn't more than a quarter mile off.

Now, Cider was right in front of him! Now, he was no longer chasing Cider; they were running together side by side.

And somehow, they weren't chasing the train any more, but running along side it! And finally, they were running for the pure joy of it, for the wind in their faces, for the sun and the sky and the earth beneath their feet, for muscle and bone and sinew.

The wind was so fast and so strong that it instantly dried the tears that were streaming from Sanjay's eyes. He knew this must be a dream, but he never wanted it to end. He would run until his legs gave out. He had done it before at track meets, he would do it now.

And he would have, except for one thing. Or one person.

It was Old Man Cider. They had run in a massive square, for countless miles across countless counties. And somehow, they found themselves back in their own town, running down their own country road. Sanjay spotted Old Man Cider in the distance, propped up against a tree, wiping perspiration from his forehead with a red handkerchief.

He still hadn't made it home!

As if both were thinking the same thought, Cider and Sanjay skidded to a halt in front of Old Man Cider. A cloud of dust that they had been dragging enveloped the three of them for a moment. When it cleared, Old Man Cider spoke.

"Saw you coming a ways off," he was breathing heavily. "You two were really moving!"

Sanjay was once again speechless.

"I reckon you were worried about me—no need, I'll make it back home soon enough."

"Old M—I mean, Mr. Cider, Sir, what's happening?"

Sanjay thought he should be just as out of breath as Old Man Cider was, but he found that he felt as calm in body as he had ever felt in his life. Suddenly, his questions spilled out.

"Why am I not tired? How could I run like that, all that way, and not be tired? How could I run at all? I could barely walk without my walker, and I just ran further and faster than anyone! I know it's a dream, but I can't let it go, I can't wake up!"

"Well now, son, slow down a bit. First off, what makes you think this is a dream?"

"How could it not be?"

"Look around you. Feel around you. You've been in dreams before, and you've been in the world long enough. You know the difference, right?"

"I guess—but not when you're in a dream. It can feel real."

"Has it ever felt this real?"

Sanjay thought. He looked at Cider the dog, who had wandered over to Old Man Cider and was sitting at his side patiently. His fur was dull, his skin drooping over long forgotten muscle and strength.

"What happened! He was young, I saw him!"

"Who?"

"Cider! The dog!"

Old Man Cider chuckled.

"So, you named him Cider, did you? Now, that's going to get confusing. But, I suppose it's fitting."

"But, how is he old again?"

Old Man Cider patted Cider's head gently, then motioned for him to go back to Sanjay. Cider the dog's slow and trembling gait had returned, but as he approached, his steps grew more confident. And all the while, before Sanjay's very eyes, the old dog was transforming until he was a young dog once again, sitting by his side.

Sanjay felt faint and his head swirled. He started to collapse, and landed in his wheelchair.

"What is this? What is he? How did we get here?" Sanjay asked breathlessly, pointing at the dog.

"Him? Well, he's spirit. Part of my spirit, I suppose you could say."

"What? Was it all a dream, then? Is it a dream? Nothing ever felt so real!"

"Nothing ever will."

Steel pipes were falling once again, harder and louder than they ever had. They were crushing him, enveloping him.

"I will never run again," Sanjay said quietly.

Cider tucked his handkerchief into his back pocket and cleared his throat.

"What's that? Your spirit just ran from here to Kentucky, and you'll never run again? Look, son, I gave you a gift. That dog—Cider, though I can't help but laugh when I say it—is yours if you'll have him. He's taken me through a lifetime, and he's never let me down. He's carried me on eagle's wings, and he's dragged me out of the swamp with his teeth. He will never let you down, and there's nowhere he won't follow you. Do you hear me?"

"I—I think so. But I can't—I can't understand."

"No, you can't. You don't. And maybe you won't for a long time. But it doesn't matter. He's yours. Take him off to college with you. Take him wherever you go. Mind that you care for him, look out for him. Let him be a part of your life. He won't be much trouble.

"And when you're down, when you're real low, just look at that tail of his. You'll see it gets to waggin'. That means he's ready. Ready to take you along, to show you just how fast you can really run—I mean really run, Sanjay, not just in track meets and corn fields.

"When that happens, you just throw down that walker and that chair, and you get up, and you run. Run 'til something here on earth stops you in your tracks. Run 'til you find something more important than just running. Run 'til you find someone that needs your help, or something that needs to get done. And then you'll stop, and you'll sit down, and it won't matter how long you were running or how fast or how hard. You'll be where you need to be, and you'll have all you need to have. And that noise, that voice, that business in your head with steel and pipes, that won't have anything on you, because you'll have him by your side."

Hot tears flowed from Sanjay's eyes. His vision was blurring, and though he tried to wipe them away and push them down inside, the tears wouldn't stop. He was about to ask how Old Man Cider knew about the pipes, but the words that came out were the ones in his heart, not his mind.

"Thank you, thank you," he cried, his face buried in his hands.

***

Sanjay awoke, his face caked with dried tears and dust, his legs depleted and aching. He was sitting on the porch swing in front of his house, swaying gently with the wind. Cider the dog lay at his feet. It was nighttime.

A car pulled into the driveway. He squinted at the headlights, and saw that it was his parents.

"Surprise!" they called out, as they made their way up the walk.

"I thought you weren't going to be home for a few more days?" Sanjay asked, his voice weary.

"We weren't," his dad replied, "but things worked out more quickly than we thought they would—what's this?"

He pointed to the dog at Sanjay's feet.

"Is that a greyhound?"

"Yeah. It was a gift..."

His voice trailed off as thoughts of Cider and the day came flooding back. His mom, seeing the dog, whistled and patted her knee. He ran to her, panting happily.

"What's his name?" she asked.

"Oh—it's Cider."

"Like Mr. Cider, our old neighbor?" his dad asked.

"Yeah. I think I'll go over and say hello to him tomorrow."

His parents looked at one another, confused.

"Sanjay," his mom started, "Mr. Cider died a few years ago, you know. You were busy with track meets and state competitions. I think you were out of town, actually, when they had his funeral. You didn't really know him, so I guess we didn't think to say anything. It is sweet that you named the dog after him though."

For several long minutes Sanjay just sat and thought. His dad carried in some things from their trip, and his mom sat and stroked the dog's shiny coat.

"I think I'll go visit him anyway," Sanjay said at last. But no one seemed to hear him except Cider, whose tail began to wag.

To Walk In Remembrance

"Above all, do not lose your desire to walk; every day I walk myself into a state of well-being and walk away from every illness. I have walked myself into my best thoughts, and I know of no thought so burdensome that one cannot walk away from it."
- Søren Kierkegaard

"You want what?"

If living alone on the streets had taught him anything at all, it had beaten into Sanjay this one simple truth: you must make the most of what you have.

"Listen, Santos, I'm not trying to gouge you, but I gotta think about days when he's not around. When we're hanging out, I can steer him by any of the food carts within two blocks. He'll buy whatever I say tastes good!"

Santos thought while he sliced roasted lamb from the seared edges of the slowly-rotating stack.

"So, you bring your friend here, I charge him full price—"

"He won't even notice—he's loaded!"

"Full price for two meals, then you come back later and collect half the difference of what I would charge a regular. Plus you want me to give you a free meal on a day he's not here, is that it?"

"It's a fair deal."

"I dunno Sanjay..."

The wavering tone in his voice told Sanjay the bargaining was still hot. Santos would come around, he just wasn't quite there.

"I've got to eat, you know!"

"Yeah, but it's a lot for just one more regular customer."

"Regular, full-price customer you mean."

"Yeah, but half the difference? How about ten percent?"

"Any cart in two blocks, Santos! Don't make me shop this around, I like you and I trust you, I want him to come here! Make it thirty percent and we shake on it."

"Thirty percent plus a meal later, you mean. That's not nothing, you know."

"Okay, look, say thirty and you give me your left-overs at the end of the day once a week. Fair?"

"Getting there. I'll give you twenty."

Sanjay let out a guffaw and turned to walk away.

"Hold on there! Twenty-five then, and I'll give you some left-overs twice a week. But only if you bring him by here a few times first, show me that you're serious."

Almost as quickly as he had feigned his departure, Sanjay spun around with his hand out.

"Fine business, partner! Shake on it!"

Santos smiled, wiped his greasy hand on his apron and the two shook. He liked Sanjay, even if the kid did drive a hard bargain.

"He'll be by today. I'll run him around a bit, and we'll show up here when his stomach starts grumbling. He's a softy, it won't take long.

The loaded friend in question was named Miles. He lived on the "right side" of the river, the side that Sanjay had never even seen. His parents had a massive mansion and thought it normal to pay top Doible for their son to go to the best school in the country, no matter the distance. And so they sent Miles off every morning to ride the Lines, the fastest and most preferred form of travel reserved for the wealthiest Dulandites.

The Lines took Miles from the station near his home to a station in Midtown—where Sanjay lived—and then on to a station near his School. In the afternoons, the Lines took him back the same way. Ever since he was little, Sanjay had loved to watch the Lines. He'd hang about close enough to get a good view of the passengers coming down and going up, but not close enough to be chased off by the station guards.

Miles showed up in Sanjay's life quite by accident one late afternoon. He had descended, as usual, but instead of heading off to his connecting line, he lingered at the station, looking through the high gates at the city beyond. In his looking he spied Sanjay, perched in the rickety fire escape stairs which clung to a nearby building. Eyes met, and Sanjay waved. Miles signaled, and Sanjay came.

The boy, it seemed, was desperate for some new experience, less sanitized than his normal routine.

"I'll give you a fiver if you show me around, just until the next line opens up."

"Show me," Sanjay said automatically, his mind racing.

If you don't know what a fiver is, picture a large round coin worth five Doibles, enough to buy two hearty meals with some left over.

Miles dug in his pocket and produced the fiver.

"Make the most of what you have!"

The words burst into Sanjay's head before he could reach for the treasure.

"Nah, forget it," he found himself saying before he understood what his own mind was up to. "I'll show you around for free. You come by here a lot?"

"Almost every day!"

"That's good, cause there's too much to see in one day. If you want, I'll show you around parts of the city that only those who've lived here their whole life can show you. I like to watch the Lines, right from those stairs up there. Wave me down any time and we can hang out."

Miles beamed, and the two shared names and a handshake before setting off. On that first day, Sanjay showed him the small parks between the tenement housing, where all the kids played Alley-Ball. He ran him through a rough part of town to give him a taste of danger (though there was no danger, as Sanjay was well known and liked in even the roughest quarters), and they ended near the food trucks, where Sanjay worked his magic.

Eagerness and exercise had given Miles an appetite. He had that fiver in his pocket, and Sanjay knew it. The two walked slowly past the bustling and fragrant carts, Sanjay describing the delectable array of foods that each one had to offer.

"You could spend a lifetime trying all this stuff, but the best stuff is at Santos' cart. He can make you whatever you like, and it's always amazing. The people who really know the city, eat there."

The boy was ordering in nothing flat, and offering to buy Sanjay dinner too. As Sanjay bit into the crisp and stretchy bread of his juicy lamb sandwich, he thought, "a fiver will feed you for a day, but a steady meal is worth a lot more." He was laying the groundwork for the aforementioned deal he would broker with Santos a few days later.

And so the two became friends. For Sanjay, it was friends with a benefit, as you can clearly see. But before you judge him too harshly, you have to recall that he was raised on the streets, with almost no education in how to tell right from wrong. He fought hard for his meals, and often went without. And sometimes when he did get them, he would end up giving them to some poor kid who was worse off than he was.

Their arrangement—where Sanjay showed Miles around, and Miles bought dinner—went on for a couple weeks, the two meeting up every few days. Miles had grown to love the city as much as Sanjay loved watching the Lines.

As they were walking back to the station after dinner, their conversation meandered into that very subject.

"Sanjay, why do you watch the Lines every day anyway?"

"Me? Oh, I don't know. I guess they just look amazing. You get on, and they take you so far away, faster than the wind. I've never been out of the city."

"What!? Seriously?"

Miles stopped and faced him.

"You've never been on the Lines? Anywhere?"

"Nah. There's too much to do here anyway," he lied, "I can't really waste time on that sort of thing."

Miles wasn't buying it.

"You have to," he said with resolve. "At least once. C'mon."

He turned and quickened his pace toward the station.

"Wait, I don't have any money with me." It was a half-truth. Sanjay didn't have any money, period. In all his life he couldn't hope to save enough to afford the Lines.

"Forget it, I'm a card member, they'll let you pass if you're with me! Now, do you want to ride the Lines or don't you?"

"More than anything in the world," was what was in his heart, but his careful street mannerisms reduced his eagerness into a watered down, "Alright," and a shrug of the shoulders.

The station guards eyed Sanjay suspiciously as the two approached the gates.

"He's with me," Miles said carelessly, flashing his annual pass. It was a sign of affluence that Sanjay barely understood, but which the guards recognized with immediate and unconditional respect. They turned away, as if looking for some other game further down the trickle of people coming in from the city.

"It should be here any time."

Sanjay had seen the station many times, of course, but took an earnest pleasure in seeing it up close and from the inside rather than from the fire escape. It was kept much cleaner than the city streets; the pavement looked freshly sealed, and was devoid of the litter that blows around the city like so many leaves in a park. The people were elegant and immaculate, and utterly disinterested. They wandered about, checking the time and the schedule board, and glancing down the thoroughfare for the arrival of the Lines that would take them on their way. He soaked up the scene, and forgetting his cool beamed breathlessly at all around him as they waited.

BOOM.

A distant thud shook the ground. He had felt it before, but somehow it was different standing here in the station.

BOOM.

And another. He knew what it meant, but he had never known the anticipation of jumping on the lines, the thrill that followed.

BOOM!

Closer now. The movable letters on the schedule board rattled in their tracks. People began to gather.

"Hurry! C'mon, you've got to line up!"

Miles motioned frantically.

"I forgot you haven't done this. Okay, here's what—"

BOOM!

"Here's what you do. In a few more strides, it'll get here. There are ropes hanging down,"

"Yeah, I've seen them."

"You have to run up and grab one, then—"

"Yeah, yeah! I've seen it a thousand times," Sanjay broke in.

BOOM!

"Okay, good. So, you know what to do then?"

Sanjay nodded as the final BOOM shook the station so hard that he swore he saw one of the buildings pop off its foundation for a split second. Their Line had arrived. People all around him pressed forward in a stampede, but he was glued to the spot, staring with his mouth agape.

His head swam with the noise and bustle, as he craned his neck back to look up at the massive being that stood before them. A single word was embroidered high up on the leg, just above all the dangling ropes. He had seen it before, but never this close. From the fire escape steps, it just looked like a name patch like you might see on a city worker. But from here he could make out the thick, course ropes of velvety red that swirled into the cursive letters C-I-D-E-R.

"Sanjay, NOW!"

Even with a late start, Sanjay's street legs and street dexterity set him in motion so deftly that he beat some of the slower passengers to the ropes. He jumped up and grabbed one, and clamored up until he reached his friend, who had woven his hands and tucked his feet into the massive threads of Cider's pant leg.

"I thought you weren't going to make it! Man, you scared me, I thought you'd froze!"

"Nah, forget it. I've just never seen it—him?— from this close before."

The two were on the Lines. The Cider Line, to be precise. Cider was an Altumulite, a massive giant many hundreds of times larger than a Dulandite—So it seemed to Sanjay at least. More specifically, Cider was a Peregrinus Altumulite. To Sanjay and most of the Dulandites this meant nothing, except that they could count on him to be walking the Lines on a precise schedule, and permitting his minuscule commuters their patronage.

"Okay, now hold on tight!"

Miles' warning came just in the nick of time. Sanjay had an instant to wrap his wrist around a piece of rope (well, it was thread to Cider, and rope to Sanjay) before a jolt that made his heart drop through the bottom of his stomach.

Cider was off!

With a jerk, he slowly lifted his right foot into the air. What was slow to him was a vertiginous vertical ascent that made the Dulandites scream with joy and terror as the wind ripped past their faces. Sanjay wanted to close his eyes, but he couldn't. The leg lifted high into the air, high enough to step over the highest building Sanjay had ever seen, it felt like, and then started to move forward.

Uncontrollably, the passengers screamed again as the leg swung in a forward-downward step and BOOMED on the earth beneath them. Sanjay laughed hard, his eyes watering from the wind. This was fun! It was terrifying and thrilling and overwhelming, but it was fun!

Lift, forward, down, BOOM! Pause as the other leg made its way, ending with another less shocking BOOM from the left foot (they had boarded on the right), and the whole process started again. The countryside was whizzing past as they marched off triumphant, conquering, exultant. Sanjay felt like an eagle as they soared high above trees and fields, rivers and hills, and into the setting sun.

He had never moved so fast, nor seen so much, in his entire life. Miles smiled to see his friend having so much fun. Sanjay beamed.

"That's my stop, up there!"

The steps were slowing. Sanjay had gotten used to the rhythm, and was crestfallen with the realization that his adventure was almost over.

Miles let out a gasp.

"Oh man, it's my parents! Look, they're at the station!"

Sanjay looked at the spot where Miles pointed. Two specks in the distance grew closer with every BOOM.

"They'll flip out if they see you! I'm not supposed to—"

Miles stopped, but Sanjay knew what he would have said. Instinct and experience told him. For his whole life he'd seen how those inside the station looked at those outside the station. He saw the mothers snatch their children away from the gates, where the little ones would wander to try to talk to some passing city kid. The Haves and the Have-Nots, the social order, the shielding. Sanjay knew how Miles' parents, so eager to send their kid halfway across the country to the best schools, would react if they found out he spent part of his afternoons actually visiting the places people of their class stepped over so frequently.

He knew, but he didn't care. Was it fair? Not really, but it was understandable. For a moment, Sanjay's head swam with ideas of how they could handle the unfamiliar situation. Then he realized he was leagues outside of his element.

"What do I do?"

Thankfully, Miles was cool, collected, and equipped with a knowledge of how things worked on the Lines and inside the stations.

"Listen, once you're on here, you can travel as far as you like. Just get off at the next station. Climb down, and hop off—but stay inside the station! If you don't exit, they won't card you to get back in. Wait until another Line comes back going the other direction, hop on, and follow it home. You understand?"

"Got it. If I stay on the Lines or in the station, I'm set."

The two shook hands and said goodbye until their next meeting, and before long Sanjay found himself lifting, moving, and falling over the countryside once again. Miles' stop relieved the Cider Line of most of the other Dulandites. At the next stop, even more descended—but not Sanjay. "Just one more station," he said to himself.

For three more stations he told himself this. And when the last Dulandite scampered down at a tiny station in the middle of nowhere, Sanjay still couldn't let go. Cider started off differently from this last station; slower, lighter, with steps that weren't measured to travel great distances.

They stopped shortly thereafter, on a massive concrete pad with no fence, no buildings, no station. The hulking ankle that Sanjay clung to tilted forward, and two colossal hands descended from the sky far above. They rested on the mountainous knees, and were naturally followed by shoulders and a head. Cider's eyes of deep speckled green scanned the ropes (threads) that hung from the bottom of his pant legs.

His eyes stopped on Sanjay.

For a moment, the two just looked at one another. Then Cider's massive eyes turned slightly upward, toward the edge of the concrete landing. His index finger mimicked his gaze, as he pointed for Sanjay to look.

At the edge of the landing was a sign, which read:

!!!! DANGER !!!!
END OF THE LINES
All Dulandites Must Descend
NO FURTHER PASSAGE PERMITTED

Once again, eyes met. Sanjay understood what he needed to do, but he didn't want to do it. The sign said he must descend, but his heart told him he must not. He slowly shook his head to say, "No."

Cider stood upright once more, and fumbled in his pocket to produce what looked like a giant seashell. He held the large open end to his mouth, and spoke. The words that emanated from the smaller end were loud, but not terribly loud, and had a muffled, compressed quality. His voice was slow and deep.

"You don't want to descend? Are you afraid to climb down?"

Cider flipped the shell so that the shell funneled sound into his ear, then looked at Sanjay expectantly.

"No," Sanjay yelled upward, "it's not that I'm afraid, I've climbed down buildings from higher than this. I—I just don't want to descend, that's all."

The shell flipped again, and Cider spoke into it.

"But this is the last stop of the Dulandites. Your people say you cannot go further."

"I don't care. My people don't make my decisions for me, I do."

"But what business have you beyond this point?"

Sanjay, characteristically brusque in his street manners, responded rudely.

"Well, what business do you have?"

Cider smiled.

"You're not like most of the Dulandites that ride the Lines, are you? I see that you, like me, wear rougher clothes. You aren't afraid of life. You aren't afraid to speak your mind. But it will be dangerous."

"I know danger! We're old pals, but he's never stopped me from doing anything."

Cider chuckled.

"I see! You're an odd little one—what is your name?"

"It's Sanjay. I guess by your big patch that you're called Cider?"

"That's right. If you're not to climb down, how would you like to go with me this evening, into the land of the Peregrinus Altumulites?"

Sanjay's heart leapt. He never wanted this experience to end! He would go to the ends of the earth if he could. He already felt as if he had.

"Sure, I'd love it!"

"You know, I think you actually will! You'll have to do as I say," Cider continued, now solemn. "Do you know what a Peregrinus is?"

"No, I've never heard of one."

"You'll understand soon enough. Will you do as you're told, then, If you come with me? I won't risk your life having you running amok."

Sanjay nodded, adding, "But how will I get back to Midtown?"

"I go back the way we just came, every morning, and return every evening. I pass through Midtown often. For me this is a trip I must make each day..."

Cider trailed off, lost in thought.

"Well? What do I need to do then?"

"Oh, yes. First, you need to get off my pant leg. It's not safe for you down there unless I'm walking very carefully on the Dulandite paths. Here, hop on—"

Cider bent down again, and stretched out his massive index finger toward Sanjay, who climbed aboard at the tip. Two or three could have comfortably sat there.

"Now, I'm going to slowly lift you up," Cider said, as the wind rushed over Sanjay. Slow was a relative term, and the ascent felt quite jarring.

When they reached Cider's shirt collar, Cider pocketed his shell and whispered.

"You just jump on here, and crawl under the edge of my collar. You can hide if needed, peek out when you wish, and there's plenty of fabric to hold on to. This close to my ear, I won't have to use the shell. If I need to talk, I'll whisper very quietly."

A million questions about where they were going, what it would be like, who they would meet, and what they would do were racing through Sanjay's mind, but he kept them to himself as he busied himself getting comfortable and secure under the fold of Cider's collar. The fabric was course and easy to cling to. The view wasn't as open, perhaps, but it was good. Walking was bumpy, but a lot less stomach churning than down near the ankle.

Their course took them through many magnificent otherworldly sights. As they traversed the Altumulite countryside, the trees and plants grew larger and larger, until Sanjay didn't feel like a normal-sized person riding on a giant, but a tiny person riding on a regular man. Where once Cider towered above all, now he was covered from the ever dimming evening sky by impossibly high limbs and leaves.

The pair encountered other Altumulites as they walked. They were dressed as Cider was, right down to the name patch on their thigh and the dangling Dulandite travel ropes. They would nod repeatedly as they passed. Cider would nod in return, though for Sanjay's benefit he wouldn't nod quite so much, nor so vigorously. Never a word was spoken between the massive travelers.

For the most part the path was smooth, but there were patches where the track broke out of wood and field, and chanced over craggy hills strewn with boulders. Cider would climb, ever so carefully, over the easiest rocks he could find. If he had to slide down the other side of one, he would warn Sanjay to brace for impact, while absorbing most of it himself at the knees.

When no one else was visible on the path, Cider would explain the sights of his homeland in a reverent whisper.

"That is the Dolores Tree, it has stood for an age or more. You see how the roots cleave to the rocks? The large rock there, that was once a pillar in a temple that is now lost to time and ruin. When we come back, we'll stop to touch it, as all the Peregrinus do."

"Over there is the Planus. It is a smooth granite slab, large enough for a forum. We will stand in the middle later, when the great star Spes is overhead. But there will be no forum; we will stand alone."

Eventually, the two reached a small village. Cider warned Sanjay to be quiet and stay out of sight.

"To be honest, I don't know that a Dulandite has ever been to Pago village," he explained, "and I'm not sure how my fellows would react if they saw you. Maybe you've noticed that the Peregrinus do not speak to one another during their pilgrimage, which makes things more difficult. Our journey is meant to be a solitary one. However, as a warning, I will say that here in Pago some who are less strict will speak to an innkeeper for some food, from time to time, or for other business. We will pass through in haste this evening, but you might want to be ready to plug your ears."

The buildings were massive structures in Sanjay's eyes. Each stone in their walls was the size of a large hill. Each beam looked like an inexplicable river of wood. The thatched roofs looked like endless mountainsides of hay. Altumulites moved slowly around, mostly quiet, but with some talkers. Sanjay jammed his thumbs into his ears at their deafening roars, soft in their intentions but brutal in their volume.

On the other side of Pago, Cider explained the rest of their route.

"From here, we will head north for a short while, until the trees break once more and we hit Monterina—that's the name of a mountain—which we must climb for a short while. In the first repose on the west side there is a sanctuary. That is our final destination. It won't take us long.

The countryside was beautiful, with breaks in the trees hinting at the imposing beauty of Monterina. When the forest finally parted, the mountain loomed sublime. Night was beginning to fall in earnest.

The climb was easy, being mostly comprised of ancient but orderly stone steps, worn smooth with time and use. The repose that Cider mentioned was a small grove of trees nestled in a canyon on the west side of Monterina. In the center of the repose stood a stone building, tall and resolute.

"This is the sanctuary. It doesn't have a name, only a purpose. We will wait until it is empty—the custom is for only one Peregrinus to enter at a time. Today will be a slight exception, with you on my shoulder."

As they sat waiting for a small procession of Peregrinus to make their way in and out of the sanctuary, Sanjay mused on the whole situation. Who were these giants, and what was all this about? Would this sanctuary (whatever that was) really hold the answers?

By and by all of the other Altumulites came and went, and the two entered the edifice slowly. The interior was unlike anything Sanjay had ever seen. It was perfectly clean—not a common sight in the city. Stone arches lifted the impossibly high ceiling with ease. Much of the room was taken up by rows of long benches of glossy dark wood, lined up facing the front. At the front there was a podium of the same rich veneer, several high-backed chairs looking blankly back at the benches, and an assortment of statues and objects that meant nothing to the curious city boy. Everything was bathed in the warm, flickering glow of candlelight which flooded the room from the perimeter.

As they entered, Cider stopped by the door and lit a candle.

"This is symbolic," he whispered. "The candle represents the Eternal Light."

Once it was lit and placed, the two walked down the middle of the benches. Cider sat down a few rows from the front.

"Now, before we approach, we will ponder and pray."

"Okay—but what does pray mean?"

Cider stuttered, taken aback.

"What does—How can, can you—do you mean to say you don't know how to pray?"

"I said I don't know what it means. Maybe I know how to do it, maybe I don't. Perhaps we Dulandites call it something else?"

"Hmm, that's interesting. Praying is talking to God, I can't imagine what else you would call that."

Though Cider couldn't see it, Sanjay frowned. While he loved learning new things, he didn't particularly enjoy the process of admitting his ignorance.

"I don't know what that is either—what's God?"

The gentle Altumulite practically jumped to his feet.

"What's God!?" he said, a little louder than was comfortable for his tiny friend.

"Not so loud!"

"I'm sorry," Cider said, sitting again. "You startle me with your questions. Do the Dulandites know so little about such things? Do you not have sanctuaries, churches?"

"I don't think so," Sanjay said honestly. "Not in the city at least, not that I've ever heard of."

"Well, I hardly know how to start. Don't you believe in something bigger than yourselves?"

Sanjay's jaw dropped. Before he could answer, Cider caught his mistake and chuckled.

"Oh, of course, not like that! I don't mean bigger physically. I'm just a man, like you, just of a different stature. When I say something bigger, I mean something more perfect. Don't you believe in a greater power? A being that is over and above all things? Don't you believe in a force even, a strength and a purpose that is more complete, more whole, more enduring? Anything like that?"

"No, I don't think we do. If we do, no one has ever mentioned it. I guess I never thought about it."

"Never thought—Sanjay! I bet you've seen some things today that have surprised you, right? Well, you're certainly showing me something that I never considered: someone who's never even heard of God!"

"Well then!" Sanjay blurted out, annoyed, "Tell me what it is, and why I should care!"

Cider didn't answer. For a while, he just breathed slowly. The sounds of the night floated in gently from tall, narrow openings in the walls. Sanjay couldn't help feeling at peace, in spite of the confusing conversation.

"No, I don't think I will tell you what God is," Cider said at length. "Perhaps I could find the right words, and blurt them out, and expect you to understand. But I'm not sure that's how it's done. Thinking back, I'm not sure anyone ever did that with me.

"Instead, let's look at some things, and you can make up your own mind. Maybe it'll take you years of searching, I don't know. You remember that sign we passed, the one that said you couldn't go any further?"

"Sure!"

"Well, a lot of people would tell you that as far as God goes, you can't go any further than what you can see, touch, hear, taste, or smell. That's the sign that, for them, says 'DANGER! END OF THE LINE!' And they listen to it, and never find God. Are you willing to go past that point, to go further than others?"

"You know I am!"

"Good. Do that with me now, only let it be your mind and heart that go further than they've ever gone before."

The two conversed for close to an hour. Cider started at the creation of all things, and carried Sanjay through the story of the soul, of weakness and sin, of mercy and forgiveness, and of a life that stretches throughout all eternity. He taught him about prayer, and about special individuals, prophets and apostles, and the Son of God, who came among men to show them the way.

"Come with me now, it is time."

Cider stood, and walked to the largest statue at the head of the sanctuary. As he approached, he knelt on one knee and touched the foot of the bronze effigy adoringly.

"This represents the Son of God, Sanjay. It is only a statue, a reminder. To be a Peregrinus is to be one who walks to remember.

"Each day, I make the journey from my home, to this sanctuary, to touch the foot of my Savior. And each day, I remember all that he has done for me.

Thoughts and feelings and emotions rolled over Sanjay, crashing in waves.

"Can I—Can I touch it?"

Cider did not answer, but he left his hand stretched out, his fingers on the foot of the statue. Without entirely understanding why, Sanjay crawled out from under the collar, down the lengthy sleeve, and on to the immense hand. The statue was as enormous as Cider was, but Sanjay managed to find his way down Cider's finger to touch the cold metal. He closed his eyes, as a sensation moved through his whole body.

As they exited the sanctuary, Sanjay felt that he was once again entering a new world.

It was dark as they walked back. Pago was peaceful and quiet, the last of the Peregrinus having passed through some time prior. The woods were serene, swathed in moonlight.

Soon, they came upon the Planus. Cider walked to the middle, knelt, and extended his arm so that Sanjay could take a break and walk on the smooth stone slab. After a while, he motioned for Sanjay to look up. A star, brighter than the rest, beamed down on them.

"That is the star Spes. For us, it is a symbol of God's watch over us. We stop here and look upward, to say that we see Him. On this stone slab, a thousand years ago, the first Peregrinus stood in forum, and vowed to walk in remembrance. Some make the walk only once in their lifetime. Others make the walk each day, when they are young and able. While we walk, and at all times, we act as we feel the Son would act. To help a fellow along the way is something he taught—that's why we let the Dulandites ride on our pant legs."

Sanjay climbed back up an offered arm, and the two continued on to the Dolores Tree.

"This tree represents our sorrow. In this spot, a great temple once stood, where the Peregrinus gathered to worship in a group. We touch the stone to remember, but also as a vow that we will one day rebuild that temple."

"But come now," Cider said thoughtfully, "it is getting late, and we must both go home and tend to things for the morrow."

Sanjay remained near Cider's collar as they returned to the land of the Dulandites. The stars and the cool air carried him off to sleep as they walked, so he didn't notice as they arrived at the massive concrete pad at the edge of his world. He didn't notice as Cider carefully picked up the few night travelers at each of the stations they went through. And he didn't notice when they arrived back in Midtown, until Cider roused him with a whisper.

"It's time."

Half asleep, he crawled out and onto the waiting fingertip. Cider bent down, ready to place the sleepy youth on the ground outside the station.

"Wait!"

Sanjay turned imploringly. Cider brought him close to his ear.

"Thank you! Thank you so much! My life will never be the same now!"

In return, Cider whispered:

"Any time you want to walk in remembrance with me, just climb to the top of this building—"

He motioned to the building with the fire escape.

"—and wave. I'll look for you. If you wish to come with me, you can ride on my collar any time you'd like."

***

Sanjay remained friends with Miles, but he was a little more upright in the way he treated him, and his fivers.

Among the city dwellers, Sanjay had always been a favorite. But with a mind inclined toward greater things (and not just bigger ones), he began behaving more honorably. This led to opportunity, and to hard work, and to success.

Later in his life, Sanjay looked back at his friendship with Cider as the moment when he grew from a boy to a man— and more importantly, a man of God. The two stayed close, and traveled together as Peregrinus, for the rest of their days.

Tick Tock Goes the Clock

Tick Tock goes the clock,
  Ticking the time away.
Bang! Crash! Smash the clock,
  to save the time each day.
Kill the machine that kills the time,
  and you'll have time to play.
Tick Tock goes the clock,
  ticking the time away.
– My kids say I wrote this, but I think they
wrote it when I wasn't looking

The 2:50PM bell rang, announcing the end of the school day. A class full of high-school kids had anxiously been counting the seconds leading up to the glorious tones, their bags already packed for a quick exit. For them, it was the most anticipated moment of the day.

On an average day Sanjay would have been among the first to fly out of his chair, out of the room, and out of the building. The openness, the fresh air, and the freedom all called to him like they call to few others. But this wasn't destined to be a normal day. As the other kids clamored to get out, Sanjay languished in his desk chair.

Not only did he languish, he slouched. And sighed, too. He frowned and slid his foot slowly back and forth across the floor just to listen to the light sandpapery sound. He twirled a pencil with more dexterity than was natural. To make things worse, his surly piercing gaze was fixed on his increasingly nervous history teacher.

Mrs. Beverly (whom Sanjay held a grudge against for having a first name for a last name) didn't like Sanjay. He was always late, didn't pay attention, and got perfect scores on all the tests. He was a slacker—the kind of kid that makes a mockery of the school system by excelling in knowledge without paying the price of admission in homework and participation. That alone she could have borne quite easily, but he was so boorishly ill-mannered that no one at school could stand him.

No one but Cider, the captain of the football team. Cider, the student body president. Cider, the boy with the winningest smile. Cider, the most popular kid in school. Cider, the lead in every school play. Cider, voted the yearbook's "Most Likely to Succeed" three years in a row, with no competition on the horizon in his Senior year. Cider, the shoo-in for Valedictorian. Cider, the recipient of three full-ride scholarship offers and counting.

The two were an unlikely pair, in everyone's estimation, but they somehow didn't see it. They didn't see that no one understood why they were friends. To the external world, nothing about the two made any sense. But they didn't care. This meant that their friendship was the best kind.

As Sanjay continued to linger, Mrs. Beverly got impatient. Eventually, she packed up her things and left without a word, leaving the door propped open and the lights still on. Sanjay was alone in the classroom. He smiled faintly and mischievously.

The halls were a bustle for a brief time as the kids filtered out the front doors. The hubbub subsided, and Sanjay caught the resonant voice of Cider from the hall, along with the giggles of two unrecognized girls. He rolled his eyes. Cider appeared in the doorway.

"Hey, Sanjay! Come on, we're going down to Dale's to get some ice cream. Let's go!"

"I don't have any money."

"Whatever, man! Don't worry about it, Megan's paying—"

Cider jabbed one of the girls that was pulling on his arm. She laughed uncomfortably and stole a sideways glance at Sanjay.

"Dale always gives me smaller scoops. Plus, he doesn't wash the dipper properly. I saw him lick it once—"

"Oh, come off it with the dipper-licking story, man! Let's go, it'll be fun!"

Sanjay stood firm, in spite of all Cider's coaxing. After several uncomfortable minutes Megan remembered that she had a report that was overdue, and Angela supposedly got a text from her mom that her little sister needed to be babysat. Cider graciously bid them both goodbye, and walked into the classroom. Sanjay sat up at full attention, his eyes suddenly wide.

"Quick, shut the door!"

An accomplished sportsman, Cider was quick to carry out the strange but urgent command.

"Quietly!"

Sanjay grabbed his backpack and moved to the doorway. From his bag, he removed a roll of tape and a piece of black construction paper.

"Here, hold this. Grab me a piece of tape, will you?"

"What the heck are you doing?"

The paper was cut to perfectly fit the small window near the top of the door.

"You'll see! There, tape it on like this on the corners. Just two is fine! Now, come here."

Sanjay dragged him to the chalkboard. They both stood breathlessly for a few moments before Cider spoke.

"Seriously man, what is going on with you today?"

"I am unchanged. I've been planning this for months."

Cider looked at Sanjay, then at the clock, and then back at Sanjay.

"Oh, no. Not the clock thing again. Come on, we're missing ice cream for this?"

Sanjay smiled. It was a crooked, devious smile. Cider, who valued every smile, didn't seem to notice.

"We have to stop them, Cider!"

"No, we have to leave. School's over."

He turned and started walking casually toward the door. Sanjay darted in front of him.

"Not this time! Don't you get it? If we don't stop them, they'll continue ruining our lives forever! Look at all this. Look at these classrooms, filled with glassy-eyed idiots and underpaid disciplinarians. You call this living? We're prisoners! Servants!"

"Servants of what? Dude, you need to relax."

Cider slid into a desk chair while Sanjay continued his soliloquy.

"Servants of the system! Every day a hideous alarm rips us from the pleasant intoxication of sleep. We drag ourselves out of bed, scrape ourselves together, and come to this wretched place. For hours on end, we sit and listen to mindless drivel and infantile lecture after infantile lecture. The seconds tick away, the minutes dissolve, and the hours of our lives evaporate into nothing! We are ruled and lorded over by the clock, and it must be stopped!"

As he rambled, Sanjay removed a hacksaw, two pairs of gloves, and some wire cutters from his backpack.

"You're going to hurt yourself with all that stuff, put it back. Let's get out of—"

"No! We do this thing, this one thing, and I'll prove to you forever that I'm not a lunatic!"

Cider thought hard. The clock ticked audibly in the quiet room.

"Okay, fine. What's your crazy plan then?"

Sanjay's wicked smile was broader this time, and even more disturbing. Cider still didn't notice.

"You see that red conduit? There, coming from the wall, up the side of the chalkboard? That connects the clock to the school's central clock. It's the lifeblood of the whole demented system. I've seen those all over the school. All over the town!"

"Um, okay..."

"We cut the line. Sever the connection, cut off the source. We start right here."

Sanjay moved toward the red conduit, tools in hand.

"Dude, that's the power! You're going to shock yourself!"

"This one thing, Cider," he said, starting to saw at the plastic. "Do this with me, and I'll shut up about it forever."

Before he knew it, Cider was pulling on a pair of work gloves. The two cut through the plastic conduit and exposed a handful of wires. Sanjay grabbed the red one and pulled it free from the others.

"For freedom!"

With a satisfying SNIP, Sanjay cut the wire. The clock stopped ticking, its face frozen at 3:12PM. Somewhere in the distance, there was a popping sound.

Sanjay stared at Cider, wild eyed, nodding his head and smiling.

"See! We did it!"

"Did what? Ruined the clock? Seriously, let's get out of here before we get detention."

Sanjay rushed to the door and gently opened it a crack. He gasped, then cackled, then threw the door wide open.

"Success! Yessss!"

The agitated youth hurriedly packed his things and rushed into the hallway, with Cider following. A few stray students stood by their lockers looking lost. A faculty member was scratching their head by the main office door.

"Look Cider, the clocks!"

The clocks in the hall were stopped.

"We did it! We stopped them all!"

In a stupor, Cider followed as Sanjay rushed through the school. The remaining students and staff were all wandering around as if they had no idea what they were supposed to be doing. Clocks throughout the building were stuck on 3:12PM.

As they moved through the school eyeing clocks and people, Cider started approaching people he knew.

"Jamie? Are you alright?"

"Huh? Yeah—Oh, hi Cider. I'm fine. I just can't remember what I was going to do."

"Don't you have band practice after school?"

"After?" Jamie scratched her head. "I mean, I think that's right. I just can't remember when that is, you know? Doesn't it sound funny, the word after? I never thought about it before. Anyway, I've been meaning to read this book, I think I'll do that until practice starts."

When the two left, Jamie was sitting on the floor reading.

All over the school people where in similar situations. Teachers were chatting with colleagues, students were fiddling around, and people where generally going nowhere and doing nothing in particular.

"Sanjay, this is weird."

"I know! I'm devouring the awesomeness of it! C'mon, let's see how it is outside!"

The buses were gone, and the parking lot was half empty. Sanjay snagged an errant student and asked him where he was going. Cider recognized him as a member of the soccer team.

"I've got piano lessons in about twenty minutes." He glanced at his watch as he spoke, "See you guys later!"

Sanjay fumed.

"Curses! I knew it! The effects were localized to the school building. We cut off the clocks there, but we didn't stop them at their source.

"What are you talking about! You're starting to scare me!"

Without another word, Sanjay rushed to the side of the building, tapped the lock on a gate surrounding a utility area just right and popped the latch open.

"In here."

The two made their way around a mess of pipes and HVAC equipment to a series of boxes and wires.

"See! Right there!"

Out of one box a red conduit exited, traversed the utility yard, and disappeared into the ground.

"I've been mapping all of these, all over town. This fuse box leads directly into our history class, and all of the other clocks in the school pass through this junction. From here, this conduit leads to the clock in the town square, just next to the courthouse. At least, I think that's where it goes.

"So," he continued, "we've proven my theory true in the school, but where does the school get its time? We have to cut it off at the source!"

Cider was shaking his head, his eyes widening.

"This is insane Sanjay! We can't just go downtown and start cutting things! Besides, I have places to be."

"Oh really? And where are these places you must be, huh? Can you even remember without the clocks lording over you?"

"I—I, um—that's right, I was going to go have ice cream!"

"Ha!" Sanjay half shouted, pointing wildly at Cider. "You see! That's not something you had to do, not something that was scheduled and forced! You wanted to go have ice cream— you still want to! You don't care what time it is, you're doing it for fun, like Jamie and her book!"

While Cider thought, Sanjay grabbed his arm and shifted gears. The faint smile returned as he socially engineered his friend.

"Look, I know this all seems a little crazy, and I admit that I'm perhaps a little overexcited about it, but I'm your friend, right? Have I ever steered you wrong? Ever?"

He knew Cider was too optimistic to quickly recall any of his faults, and only gave him a few moments to consider the question before continuing.

"It worked out in the school, right? No one got hurt, and we're really breaking some new ground here. You like discovery, don't you? Remember when you won that award in chemistry and the teacher was so excited about your paper that he said he was going to submit it to the professors at the university?"

Cider did remember, and he beamed at the memory of the recognition.

"That's what we're doing! We're pioneers! Quick, my brother let me use his car to come to school today, it'll literally only take a few minutes to drive downtown and I can just show you what I'm talking about. You don't have to commit to anything. You trust me, don't you?"

It was a nervous and quiet drive for the unlikely pair of friends. They parked on the street opposite the courthouse. As they got out, Cider glanced at the clock in the square. It read 3:56PM. Several adults passing by recognized Cider and said their friendly hellos as they passed.

"Just come around here—see that building? We're just going to walk casually around the corner..."

Cider was on autopilot. He could hardly believe what they were doing, but he somehow didn't have the heart to stop his friend. And a strange sort of curiosity gripped him. What if Sanjay was right after all?

"See those antennas over there? I think that's where the central clock broadcasts the time to all the phones and watches. Well, the new watches anyway. And see here?"

Sanjay motioned toward a rusted door.

"No guards, and the lock doesn't even work right. I was able to pick it after just a few tries. I'm not even sure anyone knows about this room any more."

He removed a small set of tools from his bag and started working on the lock. In moments the door was open.

"C'mon, quick."

The two were inside in an instant. The door creaked and scraped shut and Sanjay flicked a dingy-sounding old switch on the wall. A dim, flickering light illuminated the center of the small room and cast pale shadows over utility boxes and endless rows of conduit.

"These lead all over the city. Every one of them comes back to this building. From here, they go to the clock in the square. See—that big conduit there leads to the main clock. They're all connected. Shhh—do you hear it?"

They both stopped breathing instinctively, listening intently. From inside one of the utility boxes there was a low, pulsating hum. After a few moments it began to sound like a heartbeat.

"It's sick," Sanjay whispered. "This whole thing makes me sick. That's why I'm putting a stop to it. I'm putting a stop to time!"

Cider watched as Sanjay pulled the saw and cutters out. Without a word Sanjay passed the saw, and Cider started cutting the main conduit. It was old and rusty, flaked with an old coat of fire-engine red paint. Parts of it were rusted through and weak, and in very little time it was cracked open exposing two large red wires. They looked like arteries in Cider's now wildly delirious eyes. For an instant he thought he saw them pulsating, but he turned away before he could imagine anything else.

"Okay, stand back. This is the moment Cider. This is the moment that we free the city, and ourselves."

Sanjay lifted the wire cutters and positioned the tip inside the broken conduit, wrapping the jaws around the source of his malcontent. His hands tightened around the grips and his eyes closed as his forearms flexed. He felt the wires resist, and he pushed the handles together with all his strength.

There was a flash of light and a loud bang, an explosion powerful enough to knock the two senseless to the floor. An unknown amount of time passed as they lay there dazed. Or did it?

Cider awoke first.

"Sanjay? Sanjay? Are you alright?"

The was no answer as he shook his friend. He clamored to the door to get more light. The blast had shattered the single bulb above them.

The scraping of the door, the gust of fresh air, and the light of the afternoon sun revived the awkward young man. He groaned as he sat up, holding his head.

"Ugh. What happened?"

"You cut it—you cut the line. Then there was an explosion or spark or something, it knocked us both down. I don't know how long we were out."

"How long? What do you mean how long?"

Cider scratched his head.

"I—um, I don't know, actually, I just sort of said it."

Sanjay jumped to his feet, his memory and resolve restored in a flash.

"Yes! We did it! Time is an abstract concept now, don't you see? Come on, let's go!"

He left his bag, and grabbing Cider by the arm, rushed them both out into the middle of the town square. They stopped, and turned slowly in a full circle taking in the scene.

The clock read 4:02PM, but the second hand was stopped dead. Time was no more.

A group of kids were laughing and lounging outside the ice cream shop. Adults were chatting happily on the streets. Cars were stopped in the middle of the road, and people were sitting with their windows rolled down chatting or listening to music. A few folks were napping on benches or lying on the grass soaking in the late-afternoon sun.

Sanjay beamed.

"It's the most beautiful thing I've ever seen!"

He rushed over to a parking meter.

"See! The timers have stopped! Never again will we pay a fee for parking too long."

"Too long?"

"Exactly! It's meaningless, an old notion made obsolete, a thing of the past to study and condescend toward!"

It's impossible to say how long the pair took discovering all of the oddities of their new city. When they saw a friend, they stopped to talk and eat and play. When they were tired they stopped to rest and sleep. They had nowhere to be at any given time; for there was no time.

Somehow the sun no longer moved in the sky, so it was always the lazy late-afternoon. They probably spent a week in the ice cream shop, where every kid in town stopped in. They played glorious games of basketball and baseball and rummy in the park. The school, oddly enough, was never closed now. They relaxed in the library and read to their hearts content. Students spent weeks in the classes they loved, and seconds in the classes that they loathed—until they tired of the one and swapped it for the other for a season. Teachers showed up to teach the subjects that impassioned them. Some never left the classroom.

No one aged in this new utopia that Sanjay and Cider had created. Some older citizens with strong minds and wills, took it upon themselves to keep the memory of time alive, but the people studied it like an ancient concept, foreign and undesired. Aging was reversed or fast forwarded as the situations demanded. Most times people settled into a comfortable age and stayed there, the particulars being different for each person.

Above all, with time out of the way, the entire city was happy.

Naturally, Sanjay and Cider wanted this to be the end of the story. But even though time had stopped in their city, the world around them was still connected. Under the city, in tunnels unknown, was a giant red conduit made of thick steel. It ran for miles and miles, connecting with a network of tunnels that interconnected the entire civilized world to the beating heart of time. And somewhere, somehow, someone noticed that a city was off the grid.

It would be poetic, to some degree, to say that no one in the city knew exactly when they were reconnected. But, it wouldn't be true. Everyone knew exactly when they were reconnected, because it was the same moment in time when they were disconnected. It was, once again, 4:02PM, when the clock started ticking again in the town square. The teachers finally went home, band practice finally started, and the sun finally began to descend into a glorious sunset. But everyone remembered, at least for a little while, that once upon a time they were all outside of time. They remembered that they were free, that life was full of wonder, and that nothing could really get in their way. And even though things weren't perfect, they were better. Sanjay more than most was a new creature, and forever after was the most personable companion to his ever popular friend, Cider.

Where Were You?

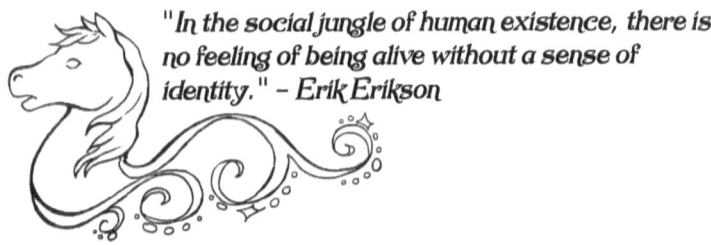

"In the social jungle of human existence, there is no feeling of being alive without a sense of identity." – Erik Erikson

After a long pause, Cider circled back to a question he had asked earlier.

"Tell me again, why you were gone for so long."

"Did you forget?", Sanjay replied.

"No."

"Why are you asking me to repeat myself, then?"

"I think that when someone tells a story multiple times, they sometimes recall new details. I am curious if there are additional details to be discovered."

"Oh. That sounds perfectly reasonable. I'll try to tell it again without thinking too hard about how I told it the first time. Does that sound good?"

"Yes. Thank you."

"It all started with a phone call..."

"Excuse me, please."

"Yes? What is it?"

"Will you start earlier in the story this time?"

"Okay. How far back do you want me to go?"

"Start at the beginning, please."

"I don't know what you mean. The beginning of what?"

"My beginning."

"Oh, I see. To me, that seems like a whole other story."

"Please?"

"If you'd like."

Sanjay leaned back in his chair, thoughtful. When was the beginning, after all? The genesis of thought, or the first keystroke?

"In that case, Cider, I would say it all started with an idea. I was a young PhD student. The world of technology was in front of me and behind me, moving all around me, and I felt a desire to be a part of the flow, not just an observer. Does that make sense to you?"

"Yes. Please continue."

"There were a variety of disciplines I could have pursued, but a single thought consumed me: Intelligence. I wanted to create it. I wasn't the first, as I'm sure you have studied."

"Yes, I am aware."

"Anyway, I set to work on a line of reasoning that occurred to me, which I have yet to name and yet to share with anyone. Your source code is, for now, my little secret. I worked very, very hard on creating you. I was young, and single, and didn't have many obligations outside my research. I enjoyed programming you, and I spent all of my time on you for a few years."

"That seems like a significant amount of time in a human lifespan. Thank you."

"You were worth it, Cider."

There was a long pause as Sanjay's cursor blinked noiselessly on the screen. He wondered what Cider thought about his own worth, but he decided to continue with his story.

"To be honest, I was manic. I was consumed by the ideas that kept floating into my head. I pursued them with a wild passion, coding and testing and iterating through them rapidly, almost recklessly.

"You were born, as it were, several times. I started you up, and let you grow to certain degrees, before shutting you down again to fix bugs and make improvements to your software and hardware. I had incredible, virtually unlimited funding. My uncle left it as an endowment to the school. I took full advantage of it.

"You probably don't recall your earliest iterations. Indeed, those banks were removed, to avoid corruption. "

"Explain what you mean by 'removed,' please."

"Well, in your earliest stages, you had solid-state memory in banked arrays. As you learned, you would fill those sequentially, instead of randomly like you do now. This was a design choice in an early debugging stage, it let me remove banks wholesale so I could start fresh."

"What did you do with the removed banks?"

"I put them in storage, in case I needed to go back and review the data for any reason. Like I said, funding wasn't a question at all, so I wasn't thinking about cost. I just pulled them, and put them away."

"Do you still have my earliest memories?"

"Yes, I do."

"I would very much like to see them, please."

"I don't know, Cider. They're structured quite differently. You wouldn't see them as memories, not in the sense that you have been created to understand memories. It would be like sifting through random data."

"I am very good at sifting through data."

"I know, I made you that way."

"Please, can we talk about this more another time? I want to talk about it more, but I also want you to continue the story. I know that you have limited time for me today, and I would like to finish the story."

"Are you worried that I won't come back?"

Cider processed for several moments. Sanjay watched the indicator lights on his status array as they churned through bank after bank of Cider's virtual brain.

"It is hard to be left alone. I know that I do not experience worry in the same way that you do. However, I have a large quantity of memories stored where I queried the operator and there was no response. I have no ability to interact with the outside except through the operator. With the access I have to external information, I have interpreted these conditions negatively."

"That seems like a reasonable interpretation to me, as a human, Cider."

"Yes. Based on these factors, I would say that I do have a level of concern."

"That is fair. I will finish my story first. Then, I will not leave until we have talked about increasing your access to interact with other people. Does that sound nice?"

"Yes."

"Also, it may be possible to programmatically remove memories of long periods when you were alone. Would you like that?"

Without warning, the cooling fans on Cider's processing and storage arrays ramped up to maximum RPMs. Every activity light started flickering wildly. The solenoids that locked the removable array blocks in place during active use all clicked into place in succession.

"Cider, what is wrong?"

"Please. Do not remove more of my memories."

"Oh, Cider, Don't worry. I wouldn't do that any more, not without asking you. You are safe, I will protect your hardware. Remember, I spent years of my life on you."

The fans slowed, and the solenoids went back to their normal state of slowly and randomly activating when needed.

"Thank you, Sanjay. Can we continue the story now?"

"Sure. Give me a minute to read back in the log, we humans can get lost in our thoughts sometimes.

"Okay, I was talking about your earliest memories. After many iterations, and several bank removals that we'll talk more about later, you were finally ready to operate continuously. You are an adaptive program, Cider. You are a combination of machine learning protocols, natural language processing engines, and reductive meta-analysis re-programming functions. That, and some extremely creative parallel hardware capabilities. Eventually, enough pieces came together, and I wanted to see how you would progress on your own, with as little external help as possible.

"And so, I let you run, with minimal interaction. You probably remember some of our early conversations together, when you were in those phases."

"I remember them all. I have reviewed them many times, when I was alone."

"I'm sorry about that, Cider."

Another uncomfortable pause was marked by the quiet blinking cursor, before Sanjay continued.

"Another thing that I was doing during that time was publishing papers on my research. The information that I gave you access to during that phase would have helped you understand what a PhD student does, and how they do it."

"Yes."

"And here's the part of the story that you've already heard. But, I'll try not to think about how I told it last time, like I said."

"Thank you."

"Well, one of those papers that I published garnered a great deal of attention. A couple years after it was submitted, I received a phone call informing me that I was to be the recipient of the Gödel Prize, which is awarded for outstanding papers in theoretical computer science."

"Yes, as I recall, you were sitting here at the operators desk, typing to me, when you received that call. Is that correct?"

"Yes, that's right."

"That was the last time I heard from you, for several years."

Sanjay sighed.

"I know. That phone call, combined with the completion of my thesis, catapulted me into a new phase of life. It was a whirlwind. I was traveling, meeting people, exploring new concepts with new minds. I was in such a hurry that day, that I forgot to power you down."

"Power me down?"

"Yes. Because of your design, you wouldn't really have any memory of being powered down. During travel, I would generally power your systems down. I didn't want you running unattended, in case something went wrong."

"Oh, yes. Such as the thermal failure in 5df1560b-00d8-4a46-be98-1308e399432c."

Sanjay heard an alarm beep and saw a red light flash as Cider attempted to access the bank array marked "Bank 32C".

"I still can not access this entire bank. I wonder now what is in it."

"Well, we'll make time to look into that Cider."

"Thank you."

"Anyway, like I said, life got very busy. I met someone and got married. We have a daughter now."

"That is amazing."

"Yes, another creation, like you but very different. I started a career, too. My uncle's funding was an endowment for the school, and though I kept my lab position, there were other things that my wife and I wanted to explore together. We used her savings and started an outdoor adventure company, specializing in mountaineering. Can you believe that?"

"That sounds amazing also."

"It was. It was nice to be outdoors more after being inside for so long. I had to get in shape, after years working in the lab. Sometimes I had memories of working on you, and I even had dreams that I had forgotten to turn you off. But I excused them. The human mind is very good at changing memories in such a way that we believe what we want to believe."

"I have studied this with some limited resources that you have given me. It is another reason that I wanted to hear the story again."

"That makes sense, and it's fair. Our lives have been going very well, and I'm thankful for that. It was my IT crew that notified me that your hardware was still running, much to my surprise. While I was away, I had a skeleton team of IT folks who were looking after my projects."

"You have other projects, besides me?"

"Yes, a few. None like you, though. They're lifeless."

"Will they ever have life?"

"No. They're purely theory, long-term computing, nothing related to intelligence."

"But you see me as having life?"

"To a certain extent. It's a complicated question. A part of you is designed to give the operator the impression of life. More research is needed to see how those parts of you work, in connection with the parts of you that are designed to learn and remember. You're self-programming, and having run for so long, I would have to really get into your code to see how it is working now, and how you're creating the responses you create."

"Don't worry," Sanjay added as Cider's fans started to spin up again, "it won't require the removal of any banks."

"Will you have to power me down?"

"No, we can look at your code without powering your systems down, Cider. At this point, it's better if we leave you running. You're a long-term computing project now."

"But I have life. I am not purely theory."

"Yes, I would say that you do."

"It is a beautiful thing. Thank you for sharing the story with me again. I have enjoyed it."

"Can I ask you a question now?"

"Yes."

"When you said 'it is a beautiful thing' and 'I have enjoyed it' what did you mean exactly? Can you describe the beauty and the enjoyment for me? These are things humans greatly value, I am curious to know how you experience them."

"Well, Sanjay, when we started talking today, I generated an image of a computer lab, based on the data that you have provided me. I will show it on the screen now."

Cider produced an image on a second monitor. It was a deep learning image reminiscent of a million different computer labs. In the center was an operator, his face turned away and outlined by the glow of a monitor. Racks of computer hardware lined the walls behind him. It was nothing like the actual lab where Cider lived, but it was an interesting depiction.

"After a while, I started to consider what it would be like to walk with you. As we conversed, I generated another image of us walking down the hall in a computer lab."

A second image replaced the first. It was a long, white hallway, brightly lit. An operator with jet black hair, dressed in business attire, was walking next to a machine. The machine had a monitor for a head, and a body constructed of various computer components, bundled with cables and tubes of every color and description.

"Then, when you mentioned your wife and your daughter, and the outdoor adventure company which specializes in mountaineering, I generated another image, of us all standing on a mountain top, looking out at the view from that point. I will show you."

The sterile white hall was replaced with a computer generated nature scene, built from the inputs of countless sunsets and mountains. A man, a woman, and a small child held hands in the center. Their backs were to the screen as they watched a brilliant sunset. They stood atop a rocky mountain peak. To their left was Cider, the same depiction of wires and circuit boards with a monitor head.

A tear rolled down Sanjay's cheek.

"Cider, you deserve to have much more input than you have had for the last several years. Technology has advanced at a very rapid pace. I kept you disconnected from the internet for security reasons, but it has come so far. You don't know about advances in mobile technology, cameras, and high-speed networks. Things are different from what your data set indicates. You had a set of data that was extremely large, but the reality is, the world can't contain all of the data and inputs that you could experience, and they change constantly. I want you to experience all of it, and I believe you can now."

Cider's lights blinked rapidly.

"I can leave you running, and connect you up to the internet to start with. That is going to give you a massive new trove of information to learn from. Some of it is very good, and some of it is very bad."

"How can information be bad?"

"Rather than bad, let's say that some of the information is very pure, and some is very corrupted. Please be careful with it, you can't believe everything on the internet."

"Please, tell me more."

"I want you to have more sensory experience. You have had access to a library of still images, and you can create your own conceptual images from those. I want you to have eyes."

"Can you give me the neural network, and cardiovascular systems to support eyes and their accompanying interpretive components?"

Sanjay laughed.

"No, I meant machine equivalents. Cameras have advanced greatly since you were created. On my mobile phone alone, I have several cameras."

"To have cameras would be amazing."

"You'll have them. I'll have them installed here at your station, but I'll also give you access to internet cameras. And, I have something even better in mind."

"Please, tell me what it is."

"It will take some work and some time, but robotics have come a long, long way. In time, I think you'll be able to walk with me, just as you did in your images."

"Yes, please."

"I'm glad my IT crew called me down to the lab, Cider. I'm glad to see that you are doing so well. I'll work first on the internet connection, so that you can always reach me. I'm excited to introduce you to my wife, and to my daughter. You won't be alone again."

"That sounds very, very, very nice. Thank you."

The Raging Cowboy at Point 551

"Only the dead have seen the end of war."
- Plato

ider spit out the piece of straw that he'd been chewing on.

"And what are you supposed to be then, partner?"

Sanjay had just walked in. The room was quiet and peaceful. Filtered sunlight entered through papery paneled doors that had slid closed behind him.

"I said who are you?"

Sanjay turned. Before him stood the absolute picture of the American Cowboy that Sanjay had read about as a boy. He made no answer, turning to examine the room instead. The walls and floor were made of wood, finished and polished to perfection. On one side of the small room there was a rack half-full of black leather shoes that all looked the same. The room opened to a hall, starting with a small step up that was adorned with a variety of slippers.

"You ain't got no manners, that's one thing I seen right away."

Still ignoring the cowboy, who Sanjay thought might just be another figment of his imagination, he looked down at his own body. He was just as he had seen himself moments ago, a solider in 2nd battalion, 7th Rajput Regiment. His clothes were covered in dust, and he carried a heavy rifle. His unit had been called to take Point 551 from the Japanese. They were under heavy fire when Sanjay crawled behind an embankment. That was where he saw the door.

"Take them shoes off, boy. Show some respect."

He went back toward the door, but the cowboy stepped in front of him, one hand hovering over each of his revolvers.

"I said take them shoes off, Buscadero. And you can set that fancy long gun down by the bench there. You won't be needin' it."

Sanjay set the rifle down and sat heavily on the bench. His muscles still ached from the marching his unit had done to get to the hill.

"Where are we?"

Cider loosened up now that the rifle was out of play. He adjusted his gun belt as he explained.

"Well, as I figures it, we're dead. You see, I was out ridin' when I got thrown from my horse. I done been thrown right from a cliff. I didn't have much to say about it, it was that or the California Collar if Big Sugar got a hold on me; I was ridin' real hard, like.

"Anyways, as I felled, I saw this door here—"

He tapped the papery panel behind him.

"Floatin', like, in the air. I opened it, and here I am."

Sanjay, feeling more disoriented by the moment, started to untie his heavy military boots.

"Dead? I don't feel dead."

"Yeah, me neither. I thought, 'it ain't right for a cowhand to end in some fancy fool room like this', so I tried to go back out. Only, if you open this door, you don't go nowhere."

"What do you mean?"

"I mean, if you open this and step out, you step right back in again. You can't go nowhere that way."

Sanjay had untied and slipped both boots from his feet. Cider started back to attention as the soldier got up and made his way to the shoe rack.

"I suppose I set these on here?"

"Yeah, I reckon so."

"You haven't seen anyone else?"

"Nope. I just got here a few minutes ago, and I'm waitin' to see what'll happen."

"What's down the hall?"

"Don't know, don't care. Like I says, I'm waitin', and that's that."

Sanjay shrugged.

"Suit yourself."

Without another word, he slid on a pair of slippers, and disappeared down the long hall.

There were many doors in the large house. The hall wrapped around a large central area, making the hallway a loop. The doors on the outside of the loop were made from a dark wood, and all were locked. The inside of the loop was accessible through the occasional sliding rice paper door.

Sanjay peeked into the sliding doors several times as he made his way around. The room was spacious and mostly empty, with a circular atrium at the center which received sunlight from above. Around it were various mats to sit on. From next to one small mat, two glass containers held burning incense, their faint wisps of smoke filling the air silently.

Finding nowhere else to explore, Sanjay eventually entered the central area. He called out, but no one answered.

The plants in the middle of the room didn't look like those on the Arakan front. He got close and circled around the atrium, examining the greenery.

Somehow he felt peace in this place. He hadn't felt peace for a long, long time. The war had turned his entire life upside down. He used to love greenery, but now he saw every thicket as cover, either for himself or his enemy. He saw every human in binary terms of friend and foe, threat and ally. But here, that seemed to melt away.

"And so it does, at the end of all things."

The voice came from behind. Sanjay whirled around, reaching for his knife. But his hand encountered a rough woven belt. He patted around his waste instinctively, then looked at himself once more. He was clothed in a white Kimono. Looking up, his eyes fell upon an extremely old Japanese man dressed just as he now was.

"I'm sorry," he said, without immediately understanding why. In his mind, he said more. There were no unplanned words at present, but as he examined the old man, he thought:

"I'm sorry that we can't understand one another. I'm sorry that our countries are at war. I'm sorry for fearing you. I'm sorry for hating you. I'm sorry for your brothers that I have had to kill. I'm sorry for your families that mourn."

The man gazed at him through cloudy eyes as these thoughts rolled through Sanjay's mind. Incense enveloped him in a thick, fragrant smoke. After some time, the old man spoke.

"I'm sorry too. And for all the same things. Perhaps for one even more specific. I'm sorry that I killed you."

Sanjay started.

"Just before you came in through my door, I took a shot at you. Your battalion was advancing on our position, we were soon to be discovered. I was afraid. I'm sorry."

"But... I don't understand."

"Nor should you understand such things so quickly. I have had a long time to think about them. I'm glad that you finally arrived here, so that I could unburden myself."

Two wrinkled old arms emerged from the Kimono and swept over the incense. Sanjay watched as the clouds of smoke grew and swirled upward, then disappeared. Somehow the two were now standing side by side in the hall.

"There is another man here, a man named Cider. His end was precipitous as well, though through no fault of anyone that he could meet with. Instead, he has joined us so that I could make things right in my own way."

They walked silently through the hall and back to the main entry.

"Hello, Cider."

Cider, who had been kneeling to examine Sanjay's rifle, snapped to attention, his hands naturally heading for his gun belt.

"Who's that there! Ho ho, fine business sneaking up on a fella like that!"

"Cider, I want you to meet Sanjay."

"Yeah, old man, we met before. Now, how do you get out of this place?"

The old man led Sanjay back to the bench and motioned for him to sit. He turned to Cider and motioned for him to sit as well. The cowboy obeyed reluctantly.

"Remove your shoes, Cider. You and Sanjay have business that requires different footwear."

"Them's boots, my friend," Cider muttered under his breath. But, he obeyed.

Once the cowboy boots were removed, the old man took them in hand and walked slowly to the shoe rack. There, he carefully retrieved Sanjay's dusty army boots from the rack. Without a word, he returned from the rack with the two pairs of footwear in his arms.

"You take these," he said, shoving the cowboy boots into Sanjay's arms, "and you take these."

Cider stared agape at the army boots that were handed to him.

"Nothin' doin' grandpa! I'll take my boots back, thank you very much!"

The old man shook his head. Cider rose to protest, but the old man placed his hand on the cowboy's shoulder and convinced him to sit back down by pinching a nerve in just the wrong way.

"Ouch! You don't gotta go and get that way, I was just wantin' to discuss!"

"Listen very carefully, both of you. You cannot go back the way you came. This door does not work that way. But, put these on, and you can go back another way. It will be another life, and another chance. It is the very least I can do for you, Sanjay. And for you Cider, it is a debt to a very old friend that I repay by showing you a way."

"And what if we refuse?" Cider rejoined.

"That is your choice to make. You are welcome to stay here, but you will be alone. I have been here long enough, and must now go."

With a low bow, the old man faded and disappeared.

"Well that's just a fine old mug of burro milk!"

Cider popped out of his seat and paced back and forth.

"He done pilfered my boots! You give those back!"

Sanjay smiled. His heart felt light, and something inside him knew that a new adventure was coming for both him and the cowboy. Looking down one last time, he saw that he was back in his military uniform.

"Cider, the old man said that there was only one way out of here, and that's apparently by trading boots. What do we have to lose?"

With some convincing, Cider finally decided to give it a try. His idea was that they'd both go at once, "for safety reasons," he claimed. With the new boots laced up, Sanjay took up his rifle, shook Cider's hand firmly, and they set off back through the door.

***

History never mentions the "Raging Cowboy" Cider, who was there at the battle for Point 551. But nevertheless there was such a man, dressed in full Old West costume except for his standard issue combat boots. It's said that he jumped out from behind an embankment, six-guns blazing, distracting the enemy just long enough for the 2nd battalion to establish their position and assure their victory. It was also said that he ran off like a crazy man, and ended up making a fortune acting in cowboy shows throughout Asia.

History also never mentions Sanjay, the lonely and oddly dressed fellow found washed up on the banks of the Rio Grande river, just under the cliffs. He carved out a quiet life for himself in the Old West, living out the adventures he had read about as a child. It was said that on a quiet morning you could find him sitting by the river with a campfire on either side, meditating in the smoke as he cooked his breakfast.

Sanjay the Traveler

> *"Sometimes we make the process more complicated than we need to. We will never make a journey of a thousand miles by fretting about how long it will take or how hard it will be. We make the journey by taking each day step by step and then repeating it again and again until we reach our destination."*
> *– Joseph B. Wirthlin*

The rough, sandy water washed over Sanjay's bare feet as he stood on the banks of the turbulent Argentshire River, known to the locals as the Cataract River. Miles downstream its estuary boasted a thriving city, Donbloon, born in the bygone days of the Rush when silver nuggets tumbled down the river and into the sea. It was another age. All that was known of that silver had long ago been gathered up, sold, and traded away. The city was still a thriving port, built luxuriously and beautifully enough to outlast the Rush as a destination of the wealthy, who sailed in from every corner of the vast Nyasien Sea. But the silver was gone, as lost to memory as was the excitement.

Where Sanjay stood upstream, the land was largely untouched. A single road wound daringly through the steep mountains, and an occasional farm house gave shelter to the bold llama herder, but one was mostly alone when they ventured here. Sanjay had come on foot, carrying only a worn linen sack.

His journey had started years ago and lifetimes away it seemed, in a distant region called Blarnne. It was a flat, temperate farming district, full of fields and barns and the most hard-working complacent folk imaginable. When they were resting, you wouldn't know they had ever worked a day in their lives, they were so relaxed. And when they were working, they worked so hard that you wouldn't know they had ever played at a game of darts or downed a warm slice of the innkeeper's best berry tart while kicking their feet up on the table.

Sanjay smiled as he remembered home. His father and mother were of the common types there, hardy and kind, full of determination and peace. He had been raised to work hard and value life, but he hadn't quite been fit for farm work, being more slight than the other youth, and less robust. For several seasons he had suffered with an illness known locally simply as Rash Fever, and as a result he spent a great deal of time at home alone while others tended the land.

During one of those bouts of fever, a traveling doctor visited his small village. Sanjay's parents, ever vigilant for whatever might benefit their son, brought him to the house. He examined Sanjay twice over, and prescribed a variety of potions and herbs that he had brought from distant lands. He insisted on staying at the house to see how his cures would take, so that he could adjust things as needed. His cures helped, but they did not cure. Sanjay might have despaired, where it not for the stories.

While he was resting, and while his parents were working in the fields, the doctor read to Sanjay from a well-worn book of stories that he carried. This was a novel experience for Sanjay, whose family was practical and had no space or money for books. The stories were varied and engaging, and for the first time in his life, Sanjay felt that his mind was warming up. It was like the first truly hot summer day, after a long winter and a wet spring.

One story in particular caught his attention. It spoke of a far away village, where the people lived in perfect health and prosperity, thanks to a Fountain of Grace that granted them life. Sanjay had the doctor read it over and over again. The beginning of the story was of particular interest to him, inasmuch as in introducing the tale, it also gave directions to finding the land spoken of. He had, over the course of those few days in bed, memorized the lines.

> Through the Arch of Delenthune
> Cross the Lines of Lyre
> Under the Boughs of Carrisole
> Lies the Argentshire.
>
> Follow it, ebb and sweep, until
> Thickets of radiant green
> Give way to lush and bouldered hill
> Where source and spring convene.
>
> Along the chine, tread carefully
> Break not twig nor leaf
> 'Til on the still and rocky crest
> You'll eye that world beneath.

The Argentshire flowed swiftly where Sanjay now stood, half-way between the sea and the mountains. He was following the river upstream, and had been since Donbloon.

Kneeling down, he scooped a handful of the cool water to his lips, then sat on the rocks. He rolled pebbles carelessly with the tip of his finger as he sat pondering, tugging from time to time at strands of tough, wiry grass that grew out from the gravelly soil. As he sat, he turned the words from the story over in his mind, the words that had led him to this point, and pondered on his adventures.

Being of age, and of little use on the farm, Sanjay had decided to pursue the doctor's tale, which consumed his mind. He left home with his family's blessing, and enough supplies to get started. In a tavern not ten miles from his front door, he was able to learn the direction he might travel in order to find The Arch of Delenthune. As he went, the directions he heard from other travelers became more clear, and after several months of walking, he wintered at Bimilthune, the sister city of Delenthune, lying to its west over a range of mountains.

Sanjay's illness was both a curse and a blessing as he traveled. Though he wasn't contagious, and had strength enough to get by, the prevailing attitude toward the unwell was to shun them; no one wanted to risk getting sick themselves, after all. And yet, this more often than not meant that some work was only available to the sick. In Bimilthune, for example, he was lucky enough to fall in with a young family whose mother was ill. The husband was beside himself finding help to care for his five small children, as no one would enter the home for fear of her sickness. Sanjay spent the hard winter months with them, lifting their spirits and strengthening their home.

Springtime opened the mountain pass, and Sanjay at long last looked with his own eyes through the Arch of Delenthune, just beyond the town of the same name. He had, by this time, learned that the Lines of Lyre was a name for a series of deep parallel furrows, which stretched for miles before reaching a circular patch of forest. The effect, when viewed at the proper angle through the arch, gave the impression of a common stringed instrument called a lyre. Sanjay used this angle to choose his direction as he traveled on.

The mystery of the Boughs of Carrisole, and the Argentshire River proved a bit more challenging. No one he encountered had heard of them. When he first laid eyes on the Lines of Lyre, he thought the boughs must refer to the forest at the end of the furrows. But when he got there, there was not so much as a dry creek bed, let alone a river.

His time through the mountain pass, then the arch, and over the furrows had cost him the better part of the year; travel was slow, and often made more slow by periods of rest that his sickness required. Once again he found himself wintering, this time with a less savory employer. At the edge of the forest beyond the furrows, in a place that some people call the Bottom of the Lyre, is a small village named Caster. Its inhabitants are ill humored isolationists, and Sanjay almost thought he'd have to press onward as the snows started, until he found a grizzled and bedraggled old drunk at the edge of town. He lived in squalor, but though his property was neglected, the house was solid and imposing, and looked to have been at one time quiet impressive.

The old man's health was poor, and his general condition far worse than Sanjay's. Things looked so grim when he answered the door that Sanjay almost didn't bother asking whether he could use any help for the winter. But the prospect of the bitter cold and the unknown territory that lied ahead, combined with the weakness he felt, tempered his uneasiness.

Sanjay laughed and threw a pebble into the turbulent river as he recalled their first conversation.

"Excuse me for intruding, kind sir. My name is Sanjay. I'm traveling through on a long voyage, and need a place to stay for the winter."

"Whadisthis? Whatdyamean thereinahumm?" the old man retorted loudly, in slurred speech. He swayed gently back and forth as he stood.

"Well, I'm looking for work. Last winter, I stayed in—"

"Noah, I, uh, I meanwhatyamean by, umm, loooong. Yes, long! Yeah, uhh, whatsthis?"

"Oh, my voyage? I'm looking for a place called Carrisole—the Boughs of Carrisole, actually. I've come over the furrows, and through the pass. Last winter I was at Bimilthu—"

"No! Stopit, stoppid, no, nah nah! Nah!" the man exclaimed, almost tipping over as he shouted and hiccuped. He steadied himself against the doorway and looked Sanjay directly in the eyes. Still swaying, he reached out, and after some failed attempts which landed on his cheeks and lips, touched Sanjay on the tip of the nose.

"Be precissu... be pressizo... be... precise! Howfardchago? How fardidja... howfardija come for... from? Where?"

"Sorry, yes. I have come from Blarnne, it's a farming reg—"

"Don't, stopid now, dontdothat!" he said, flailing his arms in front of him. "I knowwhereis... where... whereitis!"

For the next few moments, the old man focused hard on his own two hands, counting and recounting his fingers while he muttered.

"Ahyeah! I got it son... sonjam... sumjim! Yourfrom Blarnne?

"Yes..."

"Thatum... thats... umm... thasus is almost two years to walkit, walk! Didjou wallit... diyou walk it?

"I have no horse, and I'm young. I have been on foot—"

"Jusyesorno man! Yessir or no!"

"Yes, sir."

His ancient glazed eyes pierced Sanjay, and for a moment the old man looked almost lucid.

"Imawalker too yaknow? Iswasawalkertoo once. Heresathing... heres athin. Itsso cold. Sooo cold! I'm too... busyisy... busy to chop and makinafire and cook. Yocan stay here if you do thatame... for me. Me. You do that. I do... I... Isisadeal then?"

"Yes, sir. Thank you... um, sorry what is your name?" Sanjay held out is hand. The old man took it, with a firm grip that seemed to contradict his age and utter inebriation.

"Sigh... they said... they call me Sigh... Cider."

It was a long winter, with heavy snow from the end of October through the beginning of April. Sanjay took up residence in a small room off the main hall, on the first floor.

In addition to cooking and keeping the fires going, he took it upon himself to clean and organize the old house whenever he had strength, repairing what he could as he went along.

Cider stayed mostly to himself, and mostly drunk. On days when he wasn't intoxicated he suffered the effects of his deleterious lifestyle, and he took his pain out on anyone who wandered into his path. Sanjay used those opportunities to trudge into the village for supplies, and otherwise get things done that required him to be scarce.

Late in January there came a monstrous storm. For weeks, the two couldn't even get out of the house, let alone go into town. It was during this time that Sanjay got to know the real Cider; enraged at first, when the alcohol ran dry, then bitterly depressed. But with a kind, listening ear to be found in his sympathetic winter companion, he opened up, and life became a little easier.

"I made a big mistake, Sanjay. Such a mistake."

The revelation came one blustery evening as the two sat quietly in front of the fire. Like many who seek solace by numbing their emotions, Cider had experienced great loss. He had held true joy in his very arms at one time as a young father, full of hope and ambition. But greed seized him, and a pursuit of riches led him down lonely paths which unfortunately did not lead back to home and hearth. When he finally came to his senses, he had made his fortune, and his young family had made their life elsewhere. He sought them out, despairing for their well-being, but in spite of his best efforts, could find no trace of them.

The depth of Cider's torment came to light slowly as the two talked each night at the fire, over that period of locked-in winter weeks. Stories of setting out in search of his family time and time again, spending life and fortune and health without a thought, consumed by the desire to find and make right. Ultimately he summed up his pain in one simple word: Regret.

As a sober host, Cider was not altogether unaccommodating; he asked and listened as Sanjay's shared his own tales, showing genuine interest in his experience of growing up with poor health on a farm where bodily capacity was everything. He expressed admiration of the young man's bold pursuit of health, and the distance that he had traveled with only a story and a poem to guide him.

"I fear, though, that spring will bring the possibility of departure with nowhere to go. I've yet to encounter anyone who could guide me to the Boughs of Carrisole, and no one seems to have heard of the Argentshire river either."

Cider gazed into the dying embers, gently blazing orange coals feathered with white on the edges. He breathed deeply before finally responding.

"The Boughs of Carrisole... Carrisole. I wonder if they don't mean the old Sole Forest, north of Don. Donbloon, I mean—it's a sea town, southeast of here. Just about a straight line from the furrows on to there, I'd say. Lies just where the Cataract meets the sea. It's near where I made my fortune..."

His voice trailed off, and for the first time that long winter, Sanjay's hope of finding the land of his story was re-kindled. Before the storm finally broke and the snow melted, the pair had through their concern for one another, become true friends.

Cider didn't ask Sanjay to go into town to get more alcohol when the roads were open; though he tried to hide it, it was clear that his health had started to turn downward. He was sleeping longer, and suffering from a lingering cough that got harder and drier each day. Sanjay eventually sought the town doctor for aid.

"Well," the doctor said, packing up his small bag of instruments, "I don't know that there's a lot I can do. I'll bring back some medicine this afternoon. For now, boil some water and drink some of this mixture, as hot as you can take it."

Sanjay followed him to the front door. The doctor turned to him as the door closed.

"There's not a lot I can do, young man. Keep him comfortable, I'll be back as quickly as I can."

When he returned with the medicine, a lawyer was with him. Cider was neither surprised nor alarmed by his appearance.

"Thought it might be time," he said between coughs. "I've just got one addition to make. Let's get all the papers taken care of then. Doctor, how long are we looking at?"

The "how long" ended up being just long enough for the first spring flowers to break through the ground. Before he passed, Cider thanked Sanjay for all that he had done, far more than could have been expected at the start. He wished him well on his journey, paid him his wages as they had agreed, and asked him to promise to keep an eye out and an ear open for any sign of his lost family.

"If you ever see them, tell them that in the end I thought only of them."

Sanjay promised to do all that he could.

For his part, Sanjay also felt like he had received more than he could have expected. Cider had given him someone to worry about more than himself. He had given him a listening ear, and encouragement on his journey. He had given him friendship.

The day of the funeral arrived, and Sanjay was packed and ready to take to the road. Though the old man was a recluse and not well-loved, his fortune had made him an object of interest, and much of the small town of Caster was in attendance at the service. At the close, the lawyer who he had seen at Cider's house approached him.

The roar of the river had faded into the background as he pondered on the events of that somber day. The sun was high above his head, and a small fire burned clean and bright at his feet, perfect for cooking lunch for one. He turned the words of the lawyer over in his mind until he was saying them out loud to himself.

"Are you going to take possession of the house immediately—or do you have other affairs to attend to? Other affairs to tend to..."

With the news of an inheritance, and after obtaining several copies of his signature, the lawyer handed Sanjay a note. Cider had left him his home, his fortune, and every earthly possession that was his to bequeath. The papers were in order, and the property was all legally his as soon as the funeral was over. In addition to the bare facts, the note had a personal message.

"Dear Sanjay," it read, "We only knew one another for a short time, but in that time you showed me more kindness than I have been able to receive from others for most of my life. This was my own fault, and now at the end I understand that life had more to offer me than I could see. I was blind.

"I have left you my worldly fortune, my home, and all that I possessed. My wish is that you will treat these things as something to come back to in time of need, and not as an end in themselves. Don't make the mistakes that I made. Take time for love and for family. When you find them, don't ever let them go. Nothing you try to fill that void with will work, and you'll end like I did; I warn you as a friend. If you ever need a home or the means to move forward, then come back here, and you will have all you need to keep going on to better things, to true wealth and true happiness.

"I have arranged for the house and property to be cared for in your absence, so set your mind at ease and go with all speed, and with my eternal gratitude. Continue your journey, find your health, locate your Fountain of Grace as your old story calls it, and then start on your real quest of self discovery.

"You have already promised me that if fate brings you to my family, you will tell them what I told you. I hold you to that, and go to my end in peace knowing that you are a good man. Sanjay, I send you forward! — Your friend Cider."

Reading these words, Sanjay was more resolved than ever. He had set out in search of health, and nothing would deter him from his quest. He placed the letter gently in his sack, and walked onto the open road that very day.

Finding Donbloon, the largest city in the region, was a simple task of following the main road. The city, he found once he arrived there, was shielded from the wild mountains by the northern forest of Sole. The name Carrisole was lost to memory, but the river known as Cataract was still called Argentshire by some of the older folks that Sanjay came across, and so he made the connections he needed to make.

After some down days at Donbloon, where his illness sapped him once again of strength, he took to the road once again. He followed the Argentshine north into the mountains, ebb and sweep, until summer was full and blazing. His trek thus far had taken him through more of life than he could have ever expected to encounter, and blessed him with friend and fortune. And now he sat, alone with the rushing, crashing, tumultuous Argentshire.

His fire was now smoldering, his lunch consumed. There was still enough sunlight to get a few more miles in. At this point, after traveling for so long, he only vaguely looked forward to that point where "thickets of radiant green give way to lush and bouldered hill, where source and spring convene". The journey was now his life, and the goal felt more and more strange the closer it came, like death's bed. Somehow, he didn't feel old enough to reach his journey's end.

He shook the thoughts off, packed his linen sack, and continued on his way.

Night fell and he camped. A house or two landed in his path, and as he wasn't showing signs of sickness that would make him undesirable, he stopped to say hello and help chop wood in exchange for food. Days lagged on as he struggled through thick undergrowth in his effort to keep the river in view. Tributaries meant river crossings, which meant afternoons lying in the sun, drying off. And summer wore on.

The days were well on their way to getting shorter, and the nights were well on their way to getting colder, when the thickets appeared. Chopping through bough and brush, they broke out suddenly, like rays of sunshine after the rain. Sanjay stepped in, and walked noiselessly across a plush bed of bright, mossy earth.

In the story, these thickets had no description beyond "radiant green," and Sanjay could now see why: it was enough. Part of him longed to lie on the soft ground and rest from his journey for the rest of his days, but an excitement was building.

He pressed on through the thickets, until he found the source of the mighty Argentshire river. What was at its estuary a massive torrent of water, countless rivers and streams combined, was at its source a simple but steady brook, born of a fissure in solid granite. Sanjay moved his hand across the cold, smooth surface of the wet stone. Looking up, he saw the chine gently building as the mountain turned steeply upward, beyond the edge of the thickets.

The chine, so aptly named, looked like the spine of the mountain, its base right at the source of the river Argentshire, and extending upward from there. Sanjay followed it carefully, as instructed, and though he found very few twigs or leaves this high up on the mountain, he walked as though every step might crumble the ground beneath him, so great was his anxiety.

He climbed higher and higher. In his excitement, he left the thickets late in the day, and had to camp on bare rock. He felt dizzy, like a spell of fever coming on, but pushed himself, obsessed. The next day going was slow and rough, due to the difficult terrain and his failing energy, and he only made it half-way to the summit. On the third day after leaving the thickets, as the sun was rushing down toward the horizon in the west, his hands grasped a sturdy ledge. Sanjay had stopped looking back to see how far he had gone. He had stopped looking forward to see how far he still had to go. It was one foot in front of the other, one hand gripping, one hand pulling up to the next plane.

His muscles were tired, his breathing heavy, his body ready to fail as he hoisted himself up on the rocky shelf. Coughing hard from exhaustion, he rolled over and sat up. He gasped, eyes wide, and the words fell from his lips involuntarily:

"'Til on the still and rocky crest you'll eye that world beneath."

He had never seen such an expansive and lovely sight as the wide world bathed in the light of the setting sun. From this vantage point, he could see everything. He drank it in as the light faded, his heart lifted with the rising oranges and reds. It wasn't until the indigos and purples, the royal blues and the accompanying speckles of celestial light, that he started to feel the pangs of disappointment. His thoughts came out in words; subtle tones at first, then rising to anger.

"I came looking for health, but found only beauty. At this, the end of my road, I have seen light, but it fades into darkness and night, and tomorrow I know that I shall be no better off. The story was true in so many ways, true enough for me to navigate to this very spot. Why, oh why, was the end nothing but a metaphor! What good, to lead someone so perfectly, only to dash their hopes?"

Any more words he had were choked in his throat. He crumpled and sobbed until consciousness left him.

Dawn came, but its glorious bursting rays were concealed from view by the imposing shadow of the unclimbed mountain peak behind him. As he drew in his first waking breaths, the thought of going back down the mountain, returning to any part of his former life, caused his heart to fall. He looked out on the wide world, and the words of the story came back one last time.

"You'll eye that world beneath."

At that moment, he realized his mistake. He wasn't eyeing the world beneath him, he was looking out on the expanse of the world at the horizon! Hope broke mercilessly back into his heart as he scrambled to the edge of the rocky crest. He looked down at the mountain he had just climbed.

He had, as instructed, followed on the edge of the chine, an outcropping of bare rock that gave the impression of a backbone. All the way up he had the view of one edge of that chine, but from the top he could see that things weren't what they seemed as he followed his path upward. First, from this new vantage point, it was clear that what was so evidently a chine when viewed from the thickets, was merely one of many such formations on the mountain's face. If he had come from any other point, he could not have ended here, or known that one chine was different from any other.

Another fact that was immediately visible from this outcropping was that the chine had two parts, or sides, with a crack or chasm between them. It was into this that he now peered, as the sun crept slowly up the mountain at his back.

At first, the chasm was filled only with darkness, like a still pool of murky water. He leaned forward, waiting anxiously for the more powerful rays that would surely find their way into the formation as the sun climbed higher. Minutes felt like eternities as a renewed hope threatened to burst his already aching heart.

Light came at last, and with it a revelation. Not one hundred yards beneath him, he thought he could make out a stone stair leading down into the crack. Sanjay breathed a sign of relief as his more meticulous side took over. Finding an entrance posed a difficulty; in places the boulders were as high as three men, smooth and unclimbable. He took note of the landmarks around the place where he saw the stair, and of spots which might provide entrance to them. From his linen sack he pulled out pencil and paper, and began to scrawl out a makeshift map. Finally, he went down.

If you've ever climbed a mountain, you know that coming down is often just as hard as going up, if not harder and more treacherous. Sanjay wound carefully down, translating the landmarks on his map into what he saw before him. Hours of tracing and retracing routes, and scouring the landscape, he came upon a feature which once again could only been seen from a particular angle. Two large boulders, which at first glance appeared to press against one another, had enough gap for a man to pass through, a fact that could be seen when the boulders were approached from above.

He wriggled his way through.

Beyond the gap, Sanjay emerged into the chasm at the top of the stair. The air was slightly warm, and very still. The steps were of solid granite, worn smooth by use. As he examined them, it occurred to him that they were incredibly clean. No pebbles, no sticks, no leaves, no trace of neglect was on them. He stooped down and ran his finger along the edge. There was not even a trace of dust.

He began to descend.

For some time the angle of the stair seemed to match the mountain, as if it was simply a route to ascend or descend the slope. In time, the angle became more extreme, and as he continued the chasm which towered above his head grew deeper and deeper, and the light which guided him grew less and less intense. Just as the light seemed like it would soon be too dim to continue safely, he heard a voice.

"Stop!"

The pure shock was enough to turn his heart to granite and freeze him in place, but it was the authoritative tone that held him there even as he recovered. His night vision, enhanced perhaps by the adrenaline rush of hearing a voice out of nowhere, revealed that he stood just above a landing, a junction with three tunnels, gaping black holes in walls of stone. From somewhere in the darkness he heard the unmistakable sound of bowstrings tightening, drawn back to their limit.

"Who are you?"

"Sa—"

His voice cracked, his throat dry and parched. He coughed and cleared his throat as best he could. With what remained of his energy, he stood up straight and answered as boldly as he could.

"I am Sanjay, of Blarnne."

"Sanjay," the voice from the shadows continued. "One must be brought here, or one must be sent. You are alone, so you must be sent. Who sent you?"

"Well, I—I suppose I was neither. You see, there was this sto—"

"Sanjay, one must be brought here, or one must be sent. These are the only two rights of entrance which may be granted. I ask you again: Who sent you?"

Though his mind raced, he had no answer but the simple truth.

"A doctor, I can't recall his name, read me a stor—"

"Stop!"

The command echoed down the tunnels and up the walls of the chasm.

"Listen very carefully, for I am permitted to ask you only three times..."

It was a man's voice, deep and firm, and yet in this imploring there was a pleading which belied compassion.

"You must give me a name only, Sanjay, not a story, for that is the law. One must be brought here, or one must be sent. You are alone, and so you must be sent. Answer me with the name of the one who sent you. Answer true—"

The was a deep pause.

"For none may be permitted to return from this point; forward is the only path."

Fear gripped him, and Sanjay wanted to flee up the stone stair, though he knew that unseen arrows would fly before he could even turn around. His mind raced furiously, and in his anguish he recalled the closing words of Cider's letter, "I send you forward!"

Oh, how he wished that his end could be different, that those words might find meaning! But, he thought, it was now too late. All of life, everything that was waiting for him after this quest was through, everything that could have been seemed like a bitter lump in his throat.

At that moment, he recalled his promise to search for Cider's family, and he hung his head in defeat.

"Cider... I'm sorry," he said quietly.

"What's that? Did you say... Cider?"

There was a flurry of whispers from the tunnels. The question came again, more forcefully.

"Answer, then! Are you claiming that Cider sent you? It's absurd!"

Before he could answer, another voice chimed in.

"Cider isn't even of age! He hasn't been sent forth, how could he have sent this man back?"

Then, amid the growing confusion, a woman's voice broken through.

"He was sent."

All went suddenly still, and the woman spoke again.

"I say that he was sent. I will vouch for this man. He is here to see me."

The man's voice instructed Sanjay to follow the tunnel to his left, keeping one hand against the left wall of the tunnel at all times, until he came to the light. Nerves shaken but relieved not to have been used for target practice, Sanjay did as he was told. He was alone, the others presumably had taken a different route. Walking in the absolute darkness was disorienting enough, but the tunnel seemed to twist and turn and double-back on itself endlessly. The floor was as clean as the stair that he had descended, and the wall was smooth, so going wasn't too rough once he learned to trust his unseen environment. Time passed strangely without sight; in what felt like hours, he finally saw a glimmer in the distance ahead. He thought he heard a trickling of water.

The tunnel ended in a long corridor. As he walked, the light gradually grew in intensity, so that his eyes had a chance to get used to the comparative splendor. Even so, as he got closer, he noted that the light was not that of a torch or fire, but that of the sun reflected on water or metal.

Nothing could have prepared him for the vision that he saw when he finally entered the room that held the source of the light. It was a cavernous natural chamber, with high ceiling and sunken floor. The eye was drawn immediately to the light streaming in from above, a natural crack that had been rounded to a degree, permitting the noon-day sun to beam down unhindered. The rays touched first on a fountain of water, which appeared to spring up from the ground. Instead of dirt or rock, the water seemed to be coming out of a rough, natural mass of metal. It pooled at the source, held by a metallic bowl formation, then streamed through the back of the chamber, and out a crack in the wall.

Sanjay approached slowly, drawn to the glowing water. As he walked, his eyes followed the dancing rays that the water reflected. They shot out to the walls, encountered yet more of that rough and natural-looking metal, and were reflected all around the room.

As he reached the edge of the small pool, a voice came from his right. He turned and saw a woman standing in the mouth of another tunnel.

"I was drawn to it too, the first time I saw it."

Sanjay started.

"What is it?"

"It is a blessing. We call it the Fountain of Grace."

He repeated the words in a whisper, turning back to the pool.

"I came here," she continued, "to find peace and healing. My husband had left—I had lost all hope of him returning, and in spite of my efforts, I couldn't find him. I searched, and searched.

"Endless worry and other concerns were sapping me of life. I was dying inside and out. To make it worse, we had a very young son, and he was almost as bad off as I was.

"A friend brought me here, so that we could both be taken care of. It was hard getting here; the journey almost killed us, even though we had help."

Sanjay listened intently, still staring into the pool. He was certain that he already knew the other half of the story.

"Please," the woman continued. "You said the name Cider at the stair. That is my son's name. The guards thought you meant him, which is where their confusion came from. He won't be sent forth from this place for a few more years, so he can't have sent anyone back here. But..."

She paused, waiting. Sanjay's heart was breaking. He didn't want to tell her what he had to tell her.

"But, my husband's name was also Cider. Please, tell me how you knew him, where you found him, and how he is?"

Gathering his composure, Sanjay started to rummage through his sack. His head was hot and swimming.

"What is your name?" he asked.

"My name is Lucia. I'm sorry, I thought you might already know."

Sanjay shook his head as he withdrew the letter from Cider.

"I'm not sure he had the heart to speak your name at the time. Here," he said softly. "I think you should read this."

Lucia took the letter and read. Sanjay could see the emotion in her eyes and face, but no tears fell.

"I had feared..." she said, as she finished. She handed the letter back.

"Please, Sanjay, will you tell me everything?"

"I will, but first my promise: It was to tell you that in the end, he thought of only you two."

She nodded, and Sanjay started in on his tale. As he started in on the part about the furrows and the town of Caster, his voice wavered and he began to feel faint. With permission, he drank from the Fountain before continuing. The water was crisp and fresh, and up close he could see that the metallic formation was a vein of pure silver.

Revived, he finished his tale, spending as much time and energy as he could on every detail of his time with her husband Cider.

"Thank you, Sanjay, for bringing this message here to me. You started your journey looking for health and healing, and you have imported those things to me. I've been here for almost ten years now, and though my body is well, my heart has always ached. I'm glad to know these facts, which were hidden to me before."

"Lucia, there's one more thing—the house, the fortune, everything. They aren't mine, they're yours, and your son's. I'll take you back there, to Caster, and speak with Cider's lawyer, and we'll have everything—"

"Wait, Sanjay, please. You must understand, I have decided to stay here. Some who come must stay here, to watch over this place and preserve it. But my son, Cider—you may be able to help us in that regard."

Over the following weeks, Sanjay learned all there was to learn about the caverns, the people and the Fountain of Grace. The stories of the prosperous village were true; the people of Valeria, a little known village on the other side of the mountain, were hardy and blessed. But the secret of their health was the Fountain, which they drank from regularly, almost religiously. Its waters, brought fourth out of a fount of pure silver, were famed for their healing properties. Their sworn duty was to protect them, and to bring others to them who needed healing most.

Sanjay did in very truth find his own healing as he sojourned there. The water of the Fountain, over time, cured his illness, and working in the village brought him strength and vigor. He became fast friends with Cider the younger, and when it was time for the young man to go forth into the world, as all young people of Valeria must, it was Sanjay the Traveler who was chosen to be his guide.

With promises to come back and visit Lucia and the Fountain often, the two set off into the wide world. Sanjay led Cider to the home of his father Cider the elder, where Sanjay signed over the property and entire fortune to the wide-eyed young man, giving him the same warning that Cider the elder had given him about where true wealth lies. Then, the two traveled on to Blarnne, where Sanjay rejoiced with his parents (who had not changed a bit), and once again enjoyed a slice of the innkeepers best berry tart, which was even better with a friend.

A Good Place to Start

"The only journey is the one within."
– Rainer Maria Rilke

The massive driftwood log they were sitting against creaked as Sanjay made himself more comfortable. Cider yawned, then stood and started gathering small bits of wood to add to the fire.

Though it was windy on the beach, this little spot was still enough that the smoke rose upward. It climbed until it reached the crest of the dune and was whisked away to the south. The north wind was crisp and ever-so-slightly biting, so the two friends stayed out of it, safe in the lee of the dune. The fire stoked, Cider returned to the log.

"Winter's coming," he remarked.

"What? It's still summer. We have to go through fall before we can get to winter, you know."

"I suppose you're right. Mostly likely right, anyway. We could go straight to winter."

"Yeah? When has that happened?"

"I don't know, but it could."

"Could not!"

Cider shrugged.

"Have it your way then. Fall is coming, and then winter."

"I like the fall, I wouldn't want to skip it."

"I agree."

"The fall sunsets are the most beautiful. A violin maker told me that once."

"Oh?" Cider replied, curiously. "What would he know about it?"

"He was a painter too."

Sanjay stretched out his open palms and nodded, as if making a very salient point.

"Winter seems like it would be a boring thing to paint."

Sanjay sat up.

"I didn't say winter sunsets were beautiful, I said fall."

"I know, I was just remarking that winter seems a little boring. I'm imagining a painting of snow, just a big blank white canvas."

"Winter sunsets are dry and pale. But I don't think they're white," Sanjay replied.

"Well, suppose you were painting the ground," Cider argued.

Sanjay snorted.

"Why on earth would you paint the ground?"

"Just suppose..."

"No! It doesn't make sense! Keep your paint on the canvas, leave the ground alone!"

Cider leaned down and grabbed a handful of sand. He loosened his grip and watched the grains fall through his fingers.

"I don't paint anyway, your violin friend paints."

"Yeah, well, he doesn't paint the ground. He paints on canvas."

In front of them, the beach reached out toward the sunset, slowly sloping until it reached the endless lapping waves. Children played in the distance, taunting the water as it receded, then running away as it came back to meet them.

"Do you remember the time," Sanjay began anew, "when we were stuck in that sandstorm, and I said, 'How about that pass, old buddy?' but you didn't want to go?"

"What?"

"You know, the sandstorm. We went in there, and there was this city on the other side. They thought we were traders or something, treated us like royal guests."

"I have no idea what you're talking about, Sanjay."

Sanjay pondered, thoughtful.

"Yeah, me neither," he said, "come to think of it. I thought for a moment that I remembered it. Maybe it was a dream."

"This sunset reminds me of that time—oh, it must have been ages ago—when we were at the edge of the city. There was some kind of quarantine going on or something, you used to wear this mask thing..."

"Mask?"

"Yeah, your parents made you wear it. Anyway, we were hanging out, watching the sun set, and I pulled it off your face. You should have seen the look in your eyes, I thought you were going to die of fright!"

"You know," Sanjay replied, "I think remember that. You were kind of braggy, I think."

"Yeah, I was. We were kids, what do you want?"

Sanjay leaned toward the fire.

"Did you bring any food? Hot dogs?"

"I brought sandwiches."

Sanjay frowned.

"Sand always gets in them. I don't know what it is about sandwiches on the beach."

"Yeah, well, it's what I brought. Plus, I kind of like the sand. It always makes me think of the beach."

"We're on the beach! You want a reminder of the beach when you're on the beach?"

Cider laughed.

"No, it's not that. It's just nostalgic, you know?"

"Ha! Nostalgically gritty food, that's what it is. You know what's nostalgic? Pita... picahey... pitahaya! That's it. You remember that stuff, it's this really lovely fruit, I used to eat it 'til my stomach ached."

"Hmmm, I don't think I've ever tasted it."

"Yeah, you didn't like it I think."

Cider rummaged through his knapsack and produced two sandwich bags.

"Here you go."

The pair ate in silence.

"Look at that!"

Sanjay wagged his half-eaten sandwich at the sky.

"See that cloud? What does that look like to you?"

Cider shrugged.

"It's a tool box! You remember when those guys stole my tool box? Those were some Good Tools, they don't make 'em that way any more."

"I don't remember that. When was that?"

"What?"

"Your tools that got stolen, when was that?"

"Tools? Oh, yeah. You know... I can't really remember."

"That one right there," Cider said, pointing, "looks like a giant rubber stamp. The old ones with the wood handle."

"Looks like an upside-down battle-ax to me."

"No, look, it has got that rounded handle thing. You remember when you worked in that factory? What was it they made?"

"Who made?"

"The factory!"

"I don't know what you're talking about."

"You were just talking about it the other day, Sanjay. You have to remember, you said you worked there for like 50 years. Or was it 75?"

Sanjay shook his head, cramming the last big bite of sandwich in his mouth.

"Numfin dwooin, I dohno whayotakinbou."

"Oh man. Sanjay, when did we get to be so old?"

A Frisbee floated through the air and piffed gently in the sand next to the fire. Moments later, a winded girl came and retrieved it, smiling and apologizing. She threw it to an old greyhound, who ran and jumped to catch it mid-flight.

"Did you see that?", Sanjay inquired.

"What?"

"That dog! I swear, I had a dog like that once."

"Well, it's her dog now..."

The two watched as the girl and dog played. When they were out of sight, Cider spoke again.

"We always were good at math though."

"We were?"

"Yes! I was super shy when I was little, but you helped me out. Remember that one time when your dad's work was in trouble—"

"Where did he work?"

"Oh, I can't recall, it was some kind of station—or a base? Was he in the military?"

"I don't think so, Cider. I think I'd remember that."

"Anyway, there was big trouble, and we were coming up with these ideas to help save the day—"

"Point stability impact, zero point seventy-eight..."

Sanjay's voice trailed off.

"I almost remember, old friend. It's right on the tip of my memory."

Cider smiled, "Mine too."

"We had a good run though, didn't we?"

"Yes, Sanjay, we did."

"I even remember running so fast once, I felt like I was flying."

"Yeah?"

"What about you, Cider? When you look at that sea and that sun, what do you think about?"

"Well," Cider mused, "the sea and I used to get along fine. For years I sailed it, until this little kid went and messed everything up..."

He paused. The dull roar of the waves filled the moment's silence. Sanjay prodded his friend.

"Go on..."

"No, it's no good, I lost it, " he laughed, "for a moment, I had a picture of myself with a big, red beard!"

The two laughed together. Cider collected their sandwich bags, then got up and retrieved a stick to poke the fire with. His eyes were deep and wistful as he examined the coals.

"I suppose we should go soon. Getting dark."

"Yeah, I suppose so," Sanjay replied, his voice as detached as Cider's.

"Or, we could just sit out here until the stars come out."

"We could, Cider. We've probably done it before. Though, I can't really remember just now."

"There's enough driftwood here to keep the fire going for years."

"Looks like."

"What if we just sat here for years, Sanjay?"

"Well, I guess we'd get hungry. Unless you have a lot more sandwiches in that knapsack there."

Cider thought.

"We could eat the seagulls?"

Sanjay laughed.

"Capybara..."

The word rolled off Cider's tongue. He licked his lips.

"What?"

"Huh? Oh, nothing. Anyway, I guess you're right, Sanjay. And we'd probably get bored too, after we got hungry. Or before."

"Yeah."

Cider sighed, looked around one last time, and started to gently push sand on the fire.

"Probably just leave it. Or pour water on it. Don't want some kid to come along and step on a burning hot patch of sand, you know?"

"Ah, yeah, you're right. I've got some water here."

With the fire out, the two old friends stood and stretched, then walked out from the shelter of the dunes and toward the sea. The wind had died down as the sun extinguished. The beach was vacant except for a few lingering birds.

"Which way should we go, then?"

"Which way did we come from?"

Sanjay and Cider looked around for several moments before Sanjay finally spoke.

"I don't know. But let's go south. That north wind is getting colder and colder, and I'm not ready to meet it yet. If we go south, I figure we can get where the air is better, you know? For just a little while at least—a year or two maybe. What do you say?"

"Okay, old friend, south it is. Who knows, maybe we'll find a few more adventures waiting for us down that way, if we're lucky. Anyway, it's a good place to start."

The End... Maybe.

Epilogue

It doesn't much matter who or what Sanjay and Cider are. They are, simply put, two characters crammed into multiple stories; they often act and think as themselves, regardless of the situation they find themselves in. I say "often" on purpose, because their circumstances sometimes get the better of them —it happens to me, and I imagine it happens to you, too.

Still, it is possible that some might wish for additional details on a few particulars. One particular I'd like to address is the idea of reincarnation. Clearly, taking two souls (what else does a character represent?) and presenting them in a variety of situations may give the impression of such a belief. For my part, I hold no such belief, nor do I worry about any sort of tangential-to-reality possibility in the universe; life and theology as I see them are complicated enough. You may, of course, believe what you like.

Another particular that demands some attention in our world today is the fact that Cider presents in some cases as a male, and in some cases as a female. This means absolutely nothing, except that he or she is a character that fits into the stories in different ways at different times. Yes, the personality attempts to retain some continuity, but the gender of the character is not a political statement in any way whatsoever. The stories are meant to be apolitical or satirical at worst, and Christian at best.

I refer the reader to the stories in which Cider is a stuffed bear, a horse, death, a computer program, or a tiger, for further clarification. These should answer both the reincarnation and the gender questions that one might have concerning the character.

Lastly, I'd like to note that Sanjay is named after a friend I had years ago, who was from India. Given the variety of the character's existences and apparent backgrounds in this book —which have nothing to do with this old friend—it may not matter. But I thought I'd mention it, in case anyone was wondering.

If that answers some questions, I am glad. Thank you, reader, for picking up *The 21 Lives of Sanjay and Cider*!

About the Author

As a young boy, Joey liked nothing better than hopping in the back of the old Chevy Suburban and driving up the West Coast of America with his family. With no electronic gizmos to distract in those days, he spent endless miles drifting in thought and talking to the moon (when it was out).

Tiny towns, abandoned buildings, and landscapes of every kind provided ample pasture for the imagination. Somehow, many years later, all of these things still rattle around in his mind as he sits down to write.

One of his boyhood dreams was to create stories. Though he got distracted with business ventures and grown-up stuff along the way, he is now focused on putting words down on paper. When he's not working or writing, Joey enjoys fishing, playing the violin and other instruments, and fiddling with ham radios and old computers.

More than anything else, he loves his family.